NIGHTMARE HALL

THE SILENT SCREAM
THE ROOMMATE
DEADLY ATTRACTION
THE WISH

The Scream Team

and coming soon—
GUILTY

Smoke . . .

Delle swam up out of a dreamless sleep to the smell of smoke.

For a moment when she opened her eyes in the darkness, she didn't know where she was. Just that she was cold. Freezing cold. And that her room smelled of smoke.

With a gasp, Delle rolled over. A tongue of flame shot up in the corner of the room.

And then she saw it.

A tall translucent figure in flowing red garments. Garments that moved eerily in the steadily increasing flame.

"*No!*" croaked Delle. She rolled clumsily to her feet and lunged toward the figure.

It stepped back toward the door.

And vanished.

Terrifying thrillers by Diane Hoh:

NIGHTMARE HALL

The Scream Team

DIANE HOH

SCHOLASTIC INC.
New York Toronto London Auckland Sydney

No part of this publication may be reproduced in whole or in part, or stored in a retrieval system, or transmitted in any form or by any means, electronic, mechanical, photocopying, recording, or otherwise, without written permission of the publisher. For information regarding permission, write to Scholastic Inc., 730 Broadway, New York, NY 10003.

ISBN 0-590-47137-6

12 11 10 9 8 7 6 5 4 3 2 1   3 4 5 6 7 8/9

Printed in the U.S.A.   01

First Scholastic printing, November 1993

Prologue

"We're number one!"
"We're number one!"
"We're number one!"

In the darkened room, the participants in the regional summer cheerleading camp flickered across the television screen. Scream teams from colleges all over the state did splits, flips, pyramids, jumps. They clapped their hands and stomped their feet and chanted enthusiastically.

And through it all they kept smiling and making it look easy. That was the most important part of all. To keep smiling. To make it always look easy.

The remote control clicked.

Freeze frame.

Yes. There they were. The Salem junior varsity, distinctive in their red-and-white uni-

forms. They were all smiling. They were all making it look easy.

But I knew it wasn't.

I knew the horrible truth of what had happened to them.

I must have moved. With a faint rustling, the tattered pom-pom in my lap fell to the floor.

Bending and picking it up, I stroked the ragged strands gently, gently. In the flickering light from the screen, the dark stains on the red heart of the pom-pom had no color.

But by the light of day, I knew, they were the color of blood.

I clicked the remote again.

Forward.

Freeze frame.

I lifted the pom-pom. Breathed softly, softly on the blood-soaked heart of it as if inhaling the scent of some fatal flower.

I caressed the deliciously death-stained strands delicately.

Had the Salem junior varsity cheerleaders been smiling when they died?

Would the new scream team make death look easy?

I clicked the remote one last time.

The screen went dark.

Freeze frame . . .

forever.

Chapter 1

"I'm dying," Delle Arlen gasped, clutching her throat. She staggered. Lurched sideways. Dropped heavily to her hands and knees.

A dark shadow fell across the grass in front of her.

A voice above her spoke.

"Get up!" the voice rasped harshly.

The girl in the baggy white shorts and the skintight T-shirt turned her head to one side to stare out of the corner of her eyes at the figure towering above her.

Anyone could see that Delle was pretty. Beautiful, in fact.

But right now her face was red, her eyes glazed. She was obviously more familiar with fun than with pain.

"Get up or give up," the voice said. "Do you hear me?"

Delle got to her knees. Forced herself unsteadily to her feet to face the cheerleading coach. "I hear you," she said. "And I'm *not* a quitter."

Turning on her heel, she began to run.

Far ahead of her, other figures straggled around the track in the first light of dawn. Although it was early, the heat already shimmered up off the cinders. It was going to be another scorching day. Unusually hot for early fall in that part of the country.

Regrettably hot for early fall for that particular time and place.

Because it was the first day of cheerleading tryouts at Salem University.

The coach walked back to the bleachers and sat down to watch the cheerleading hopefuls circle the track. It was, of course, too early to tell anything about any of the candidates yet. They'd just arrived the night before. She'd posted a training schedule at Abbey House, the dorm they'd come to from all over campus, to stay for the week of tryouts. But she'd only just met them face to face an hour earlier, at 6:00 A.M. that morning. They'd come hopefully across the grass toward old Peabody Gym, some sleepy, some clearly early risers, all trying to look like they were The Ones. Winners. The Cheerleaders To Be.

She'd wasted no time before lining them up

in a sort of boot camp formation in the sun-parched center of the old track by the gym.

"Good morning," she'd said then, briskly. And waited.

It had taken them a moment, but they'd caught on and answered, "Good morning."

Acknowledging it with a small nod, she'd said, "These are the cheerleading tryouts for the junior varsity squad of Salem University. Two people who were original members of the junior varsity will be on the new team this year and I will be choosing six additional cheerleaders at the end of this week. Until then, you will be working out, learning skills, demonstrating your teamwork abilities, and showing me why you are qualified to be a cheerleader. The final choice will not be made just on the final day, but on what I observe here all week."

The coach had taken a deep breath and looked at her recruits. There was so much she wanted to tell them. But how?

"Cheerleading is *not* about popularity or looks or partying. It is a sport. A cheerleader has as much right to be proud of being a finely tuned athlete as a football player or a basketball player or any of the other teams that the cheering squad supports. You are athletes, supporting other athletes. It is up to you to measure up, athletically, to the other athletes, who are your colleagues."

She'd stopped. They'd looked at her blankly.

"Oh, well," she'd said almost to herself. "I'm new and you're new. These things take time."

Raising her voice, she'd concluded, "Cheerleading takes talent, skill, athleticism, and practice. My cheerleaders are, first of all, athletes. They work out as do other athletes. They observe training. They behave. They give their jobs as cheerleaders one hundred and ten percent. If they do not, they are benched.

"Do I make myself clear?"

The tone of her voice had said she didn't expect any questions. No one had asked any.

Briefly she had introduced the two cocaptains, Marla Pines and Rory Hanahama, and the former cheerleader now on crutches, who would be helping her with the tryouts, Jennifer Li. The thought of those three made her pause. Something wasn't right about that whole setup . . .

Oh, well. She'd get to the bottom of it.

The first hour of training was almost over now. As soon as everyone finished their three-mile run they'd have an hour and a half to eat breakfast or try to rest for the next session, which lasted from nine until twelve. Then another hour-and-a-half break and three-and-a-half hours of training again.

At night, there would be cheers to memorize.

Coach Truite smiled ruefully. She knew she came across as a martinet, almost a fanatic. But she considered the pose part of her job. Too many people thought cheerleading was some sort of spectator sport. Too many people went out for it for the glamour, the popularity.

She was going to prove them wrong.

She raised her megaphone. "Keep moving," she shouted through it. "Get those bodies going!"

Susan Worth stared at the ceiling of the old dormitory room. She'd thought she would pass out from exhaustion the moment she'd lain down in the narrow, lumpy bed, but in spite of the fact that every muscle in her body ached, her mind kept racing furiously.

Confused images of the day swam before her eyes: staggering at dawn down the worn, wooden-floored hall of the dorm toward the equally ancient bathroom. The groan of the old pipes as she twisted on the shower faucet. The sleep-glazed eyes and puffy faces of the other girls on the floor whom she met going in and out of the communal bathroom.

She turned, seeking in vain for a more comfortable position, and groaned as her muscles protested. She groaned, too, at the thought of how carefully she'd picked out the clothes to wear on the first morning of the cheerleading tryouts session at Salem University. She'd always believed in being pulled together, prepared outwardly, at least, for whatever was ahead. It had always given her confidence a little extra boost.

But her confidence had ebbed as she'd fallen into the rigidly straight lines and stood at what amounted to attention under the coach's inspection. She had not been prepared, outwardly or inwardly, for the day that had just passed.

Was this really what college was going to be like? The big adventure she'd so looked forward to? Was it going to be a series of days of being unprepared, of being not quite ready, of not knowing what was expected until it was almost too late and then having to scramble to keep up?

At first she'd thought she was catching on. When she'd gotten the cheerleading tryout notice in her campus mailbox, she'd thought that it would be the icing on the cake. Just what she needed to really fit in. She'd been a good cheerleader in high school. How hard could it be now?

But all the confidence she'd brought to Salem, all the confidence she'd brought to Abbey House (odd that they all had to stay in the same dorm during the tryouts. Part of the coach's fanatical emphasis on teamwork?) had all begun to drain away. No, *sweat* away, during the long, grueling hours of the first day of tryout practice.

And everyone else seemed so good. So self-confident.

But she had to win. She *had* to. No matter what it took. The idea of failing, of people laughing at her, pointing at her, was unbearable.

Almost as unbearable as being a nobody at this big new school.

The small figure on the bed shifted restlessly. And groaned softly again. Susan Worth was not used to being unprepared. She wasn't used to coming in second.

And she never, ever cried.

Which is why she closed her eyes at last, even though she wasn't sleepy. It was harder for the tears to spill over that way.

Delle huddled in the bay window of the first floor lounge, looking out at the other girls and guys sprawled around the room. It was an elegant room whose beautiful oak paneling and thick plaster walls gave it the feel of another, more formal era despite the jarringly modern furniture scattered over worn Oriental carpets.

Shifting, trying to find a more comfortable position, Delle grimaced. Every time she moved, something hurt.

A girl sprawled in the chair next to the window, her maroon-burnished black hair in a thousand tiny braids spread over the back of it, looked at Delle and made a sympathetic face.

Delle tried to turn her grimace into a smile. She wasn't sure she succeeded.

"They say the second day is harder," the girl said, fingering a crystal suspended on a thin silver chain at the base of her neck. "The third day it gets better."

"I should last so long," said Delle. The girl in braids nodded.

Delle realized that she was only half-kidding about making it to the third day of the tryouts. After all, it didn't look — or feel — very promising for the second day tomorrow.

Had cheerleading ever been this hard back home in Cedar Bluffs? All she could remember were the cheering crowds, the warm camaraderie among her team members. The fun.

A girl with cropped blonde hair, a knockout

figure, and pale blue eyes had just walked into the room with the air of someone who expected to be noticed. As she spoke to a group of people nearest the door Delle remembered who she was: Marla Pines, one of the co-captains. Although how the girl had become a co-captain without even trying out was puzzling.

Delle frowned, then shifted again. Ugh, that hurt. No, she'd never been so sore in the whole time — all through junior high and high school — she'd been a cheerleader. She'd loved every minute of it and she'd jumped at the chance to try out for the Salem University junior varsity. If she made the team, she decided, her freshman year at Salem would be just about perfect.

In fact, the only thing that would make it more perfect would be just the right guy. Not somebody like Warren. Serious, let's-get-married-after-high school Warren. When he'd asked her the night of the senior prom, she'd been so surprised she'd laughed.

That had hurt Warren's feelings. It had made a very unhappy ending to an otherwise terrific evening.

But how could he ask her to marry him? When he knew how excited she was about going to Salem? When there was a whole world out there waiting to be explored? When she wasn't in love with him and he wasn't in love with her?

Warren had forgiven her. Then he'd stopped speaking to her, although she kept seeing him around. Almost as if he were lurking, watching. Following her.

But she must have been wrong about that. Because three months later, right before she left for Salem, he'd left. Just packed up his old truck with a camper on the back and taken off.

So that made twice Warren had surprised her in all the time they had been going together. Once when he'd asked her to marry him, and the second time when he'd just disappeared.

But then, he'd always been a little strange, in spite of his all-American appearance.

She wondered where he was now . . .

Marla Pines spoke. Her slightly high-pitched voice carried through the room and jerked Delle's attention back to the present with the last two words.

". . . dead cheerleaders?" Marla paused dramatically, looking around the room to watch the effect of her words.

A profound silence fell.

"No, I guess they didn't tell you about that when they gave you all the information about these tryouts, did they?" Marla raised her eyebrows. "They didn't tell you *why* they had to pick six new members of the junior varsity."

Marla reached up to fluff her short, upswept golden mane. Several rings glinted on her fingers and heart-shaped trinkets dangled at her ears.

"What my — beautiful — co-captain is trying to say," a voice interrupted, "is that she and I became co-captains by default. A sort of *fatal* default." A tall, athletic boy lounged into the room and propped himself against the door jamb. He folded his arms and smiled sweetly at Marla.

A series of expressions chased themselves across Marla's carefully made-up face: surprise, annoyance, calculation, and then a coy smile. "Rory," she said at last, noncommittally.

"Wowwww," breathed Delle. Why hadn't she noticed him earlier? She looked up and realized that the girl in the braids had heard her and was smiling.

Delle felt the blush staining her cheeks, but she couldn't help thinking, I could have some fun with him. . . .

The dark-haired girl next to Delle said, "I'd like to know what's going on, if you don't mind. You were saying, about the cheerleading try-outs?"

"Just this," said Marla, the smile fixed on

her face, her eyes fixed on Rory. It gave Delle an eerie feeling, as if she were watching a performance in a play. "Practically the entire junior varsity team was killed in a freak bus accident this summer."

A gasp went around the room as Marla continued, "All except me and Rory here. And Jennifer Li. I'd gotten the flu. So I left camp early — two days before. Jennifer was on the bus, but was thrown clear — *somehow*. They found her yards and yards away. At first they thought she was dead, too. She said she didn't remember a thing. And then there's Rory."

Marla stopped. She was watching Rory. And suddenly, it seemed as if everyone in the room was, too.

Rory's expression darkened and he unfolded his arms and stood up straight.

Don't let her get to you like that, thought Delle. Can't you see it's what she wants?

The two, Marla and Rory, staring hard at one another, might have been alone in the room.

Then Rory said, "And I caught a ride with a friend from State U."

"At the last minute," added Marla sweetly.

Delle couldn't stand it anymore. "What are you saying?" she challenged Marla.

Marla looked slowly around the room, letting

her gaze come to rest on Delle at last. For a long, measured moment, the two girls studied each other.

Then Marla said, "What I'm saying is that some people say that it wasn't an accident. That someone meant for the team — or someone on the team — to die.

"That the Salem junior varsity was *murdered*."

Chapter 2

"That's not true," said Rory angrily.

"Prove it," said Marla. "What about the brakes? The police said they 'couldn't rule out the possibility that someone had tampered with the brakes.' Remember, Rory?"

A harsh voice cut across the rising babble of voices in the room.

"No one will prove anything!" Coach Truite strode into the room with military precision, and somehow Marla faded into the crowd. Rory stood his ground and Coach Truite turned to face the others. Her eyes narrowed.

"I will have no rumors, no backbiting, no trouble. I am picking a *team*. The individuals comprising that team must work together efficiently. I will have no one on my team who is not a team player. Is that clear?" She stared hard for a moment at Marla, who quickly turned her head away. "I said, is that clear?"

Subdued murmurs of assent answered the coach.

She seemed satisfied. The stern look on her face relaxed, and, although she didn't smile, she looked less forbidding than she had all day.

"For those of you who are unaware of the tragedy to which Ms. Pines, I believe, was referring . . ."

"Woo," whispered the girl in the chair next to Delle. "She doesn't miss a *thing*."

". . . returning from the annual Regional Cheerleading Camp and Competition at the end of June. The new junior varsity team, chosen last spring, had done very well. The bus in which they were riding apparently skidded out of control. There was one survivor, Jennifer Li, whom you met today, and who has graciously consented to help with the tryouts, although she has decided against returning to the team. Two other junior varsity members, Marla Pines and Rory Hanahama, were not on the bus. As the only remaining members of the original junior varsity team, they will be the co-captains this year, and, as I said earlier today, will be assisting me with the tryouts. Now, are there any questions?"

No one moved. No one dared speak.

The coach smiled at last, a resigned smile. Then she shrugged. "Well then, I believe I posted lights out at eleven o'clock. It is now ten-thirty. Six-thirty tomorrow morning will come very early. Let me suggest to you that you begin your preparations for retiring *now*."

A general scramble ensued as the crowd in the room tried to make itself disappear as quickly and inconspicuously as possible, the boys to the first floor of Abbey House and the girls to the second. The third floor hadn't been needed and had remained closed as, apparently, it usually was.

"Mojo," volunteered the girl with the braids, falling into step beside Delle as she labored up the stairs. "My name's Morgana, but everybody calls me Mojo. Some show tonight, huh?"

"Yeah," said Delle glumly. Then she said, "Oh, sorry. I'm Delle Arlen."

Mojo nodded. They'd reached the second floor and were headed down the hall. "This building's like something out of an old movie, isn't it? You know, the creepy kind, with things living under the stairs and all."

"Puh-*leeze*," Delle laughed, and then winced. Was it possible for her whole body to hurt even when she laughed? Apparently so.

" 'Course it's not as major creepy as that old off-campus accommodation I saw on the way in . . . Nightingale Hall, the sign said. I'm sorta sensitive to vibrations, and I'm telling you, it gave me *bad* signals. Y'know?"

Delle frowned. "I've heard of Nightingale Hall . . ."

"You shoulda. A girl killed herself there last spring. Hung herself. Now they say it's *haunted*. No one calls it Nightingale Hall anymore. They call it *Nightmare* Hall. Get it?" Mojo conveyed the information with such relish that Delle was taken aback. But before she could get a word in edgewise, Mojo went on. "This is my dogtrot." Mojo pushed open the door to one of the narrow single rooms which made up Abbey House. "Where's yours?"

"By the fire exit stairs," said Delle.

"Not a bad place to be in an old heap like this," said Mojo. "Come and go when ya please, without bein' seen. Or maybe a quick escape from anything . . . supernatural. Decent." She paused. "Although the Lady in Red is actually the ghost of Peabody Gym, not Abbey House."

About to lift her hand in a casual farewell salute, Delle stopped short. "What are you talking about?"

"The Lady in Red. The Red Lady. The girl who was burned to death in Peabody Gym."

"Peabody Gym," repeated Delle stupidly.

Mojo nodded. "Y'know, the gym where we're practicing? When we're not being tortured to death outside on the track?"

Seeing the apprehension on Delle's face, Mojo was immediately contrite. "Geez, I'm sorry. I wouldn'a mentioned it. Only I thought everybody knew about it. I mean, people were talkin' about it today an' all."

Delle waited, and Mojo went on: "The Red Lady is a girl who got trapped in the old gym, back when Salem University was divided into two schools, one for men and one for women. This was the women's school, y'know? Abbey House and Peabody Gym are the only part that's left. They only use this old heap for conferences and stuff, but the gym is still used by the scream teams and the smaller sports groups, the fencing team and like that . . ."

In exasperation, Delle almost shouted, "*Mojo! Who* is the Red Lady???"

"Oh. Sorry. Okay. So the old gym, which was also called Peabody Gym, burned down back at the turn of the century. And one of the girls who was in it got trapped and couldn't get out. So now she like appears, y'know? When something terrible is going to happen."

"So you're saying Peabody Gym is haunted?" The idea struck Delle as funny for some reason. Maybe she was slaphappy from exhaustion. "What does she wear? Old gym shorts? Bloomers? Not *red* bloomers! How shocking!"

"No! Red for *fire*! Listen," said Mojo,

seriously, "I believe in that stuff!"

"I *don't*," replied Delle firmly. It was almost eleven. "I'm going to bed. See you tomorrow, Mojo."

Mojo stepped into the shadowy doorway of her room. "Listen," she repeated.

"What?" said Delle.

"They're saying that the Red Lady appeared last summer. They were having some kind of math conference rooms. And the people who were staying here in Abbey House, the ones whose rooms faced across Abbey Lawn to Peabody Gym? They saw her. Right before the cheerleaders died." Mojo nodded once, for emphasis.

"I don't believe in — " Delle began, but she didn't get to finish. Mojo had already shut the door to her room.

The lights overhead flicked off and on once.

Startled, Delle turned. Marla Pines stood by the stairs, her hand on the switch. How long had she been there? Had she been listening in on their conversation?

Marla flicked the switch again. "Lights out in five minutes," she announced staring intently at Delle. Then she turned abruptly, leaving Delle alone in the hallway.

Unsettled, more upset than she liked to admit by Mojo's revelations, Delle made her way slowly down to her room.

Mindful of her aching muscles, Delle eased out of her clothes and into her nightshirt and lay down carefully on the narrow, lumpy mattress. Not until she'd pulled the covers up did she realize that she'd left her window open.

She was too tired and too sore to get up and close it. Oh well, it didn't matter. It was still warm out. And she was on the second floor, so no one would be leaping through the window.

Besides, the sounds of the crickets and the heavy smell of freshly cut grass on Abbey Lawn were familiar and comforting.

Delle closed her eyes, expecting to fall asleep immediately. But she couldn't. She kept thinking about the cheerleaders who'd died. About the Lady in Red. About the poor girl who'd hanged herself in Nightingale Hall.

Nightmare Hall, she repeated to herself silently. Ugh.

She felt an unexpected gratitude for her room over in the Quad, which she looked forward to returning to at the end of the week. No ghosts there, at least.

Finally she fell asleep.

Smoke.

Delle swam up out of a dreamless sleep to the smell of smoke.

For a moment when she opened her eyes in

the darkness, she didn't know where she was. Just that she was cold. Freezing cold. And that her room smelled of smoke.

Then she realized that there really *was* smoke.

Accompanied by the strangely merry sound of flames crackling, burning.

With a gasp, Delle rolled over. A tongue of flame shot up in the corner of the room.

"No," she gasped.

And then she saw it.

A tall translucent figure in flowing red garments. Garments that moved eerily in the steadily increasing flame.

"*No!*" croaked Delle. She rolled clumsily to her feet and lunged toward the figure.

It stepped back toward the door.

And vanished.

Delle grabbed the door handle to her room and cried out. The handle was freezing. So cold it burnt her hand. Almost instinctively, she twisted the tail of her nightshirt around her hand and grabbed the doorknob again.

It wouldn't turn.

Out of the corner of her eye, she saw the flames leap up, growing, licking up the dark.

She was trapped.

Chapter 3

"NOOO," screamed Delle. It was a nightmare. It had to be.

But it wasn't.

Frantically Delle pulled on the door. It wouldn't give.

"Help me!" she cried. "Help! Fire!"

The flames hissed and snaked upward.

She couldn't breathe. Smoke filled the room as the flames leaped and danced.

Delle looked wildly around.

Grabbing the blanket folded across the foot of her bed, she began to beat frantically at the flames.

Almost as if they were alive, they fought against being smothered. They fought to engulf her. To take her life and make it theirs.

The heat singed her hair. She smelled it burning, smelled the cotton of the blanket as it scorched in her hands.

Blindly now, panicked, she lashed out at the flames again and again. She couldn't breathe.

She was going to die.

And then, suddenly, the door burst open and a tall figure began to spray white foam from the fire extinguisher. With malevolent hisses and whispers the flames began to die.

Someone flipped the light switch. Hands grabbed Delle, pulling her back and demanding, "Are you okay?" It was Marla Pines.

"F-fine . . ." Delle stammered.

Someone else said, "Is it a fire? Is it out?"

Another voice answered, "Yes. Open a window. Let's get some fresh air in here."

"It was the trash can," said Marla, pointing.

"What happened?" demanded an authoritarian voice, and Delle, who'd been staring blankly at the twisted, blackened metal trash can that had been in one corner of her room, turned to face Coach Truite.

"Well?" said the Coach.

"I-I don't know," Delle said. Just past the coach's shoulder she saw Mojo, her strange silver-green eyes alight with excitement. And, to Delle's embarrassment, she saw most of the rest of the dorm as well — including the guys from the first floor.

Oh, no, she groaned inwardly.

"Well?" said Coach Truite again, impatiently.

"I don't know what happened," said Delle. "One minute I was asleep and the next minute I woke up and smelled smoke and there was fire."

"Were you smoking?" demanded Coach Truite. "Did you put a cigarette out in the garbage can?"

"No!" said Delle indignantly. "I don't smoke!"

Silently, the coach leaned over and poked in the still smoldering mass, seemingly unaware of the possibility of getting burned. Delle caught a glimpse of a blackened newspaper. Then the coach straightened up, holding a cigarette butt in Delle's face.

Delle's mouth dropped open. How had that gotten there? And when? Had someone who'd lived in the room before left it?

No, it wasn't possible. Was it? How long could a cigarette butt smolder before it started a fire?

Trying to get control of herself, Delle finally blurted out, "I don't smoke, I tell you! It's not mine. And I hadn't been reading the newspaper either, for that matter."

The coach looked totally disgusted. "You'd better *not* smoke! How you destroy yourself on your own time is your business. But *my* cheerleaders keep training just like any other atheletes. Smoking is *not* allowed."

Delle said, desperately, "I don't smoke, I tell you. Someone was in my room . . ."

"What's this?" Coach Truite, who'd been in the act of turning away, swung back around to face Delle.

"I saw someone. In the door of my room. Right when I woke up."

"Who?"

"I don't know. I couldn't see her face . . . she just disappeared. And then the door wouldn't open — "

"She?"

"Yes. She was in a long red dress . . ."

The coach's eyes snapped. *"What?"*

"The Lady in Red," Mojo blurted out. "She was *here!*"

"Quiet," ordered Coach Truite without turning her head. She glared at Delle. "This pathetic attempt to cover up the fact that your careless and disobedient smoking caused a fire in your room — "

"No!" cried Delle, shrinking back from the coach's fury.

But before Coach Truite could continue, the whispering, watching crowd outside Delle's door parted. Limping painfully on her crutches,

Jennifer Li dragged herself to the door of Delle's room and stopped.

"Y-you saw her? The Lady in Red?" Jennifer said, harshly.

Delle nodded.

Twisting awkwardly, Jennifer looked down at the charred remains of the metal wastebasket, then at Delle. Then she looked at Coach Truite.

Jennifer's eyes were huge and her creamy complexion had a sickly green hue. She looked as if she were about to faint as she murmured, seemingly to herself, "They saw her too. Last spring in the gym. Before . . . before the accident. And now you saw her. Here! She's never been seen outside the gym before."

"Jennifer," said the coach.

Oblivious, Jennifer went on, her voice rising. "Oh, no! No, no, no! She's trying to tell us, trying to warn us. Just like she did then!"

Jennifer's voice rose to a shriek. "She's warning us! She's warning us. It's the cheerleaders. It's the cheerleaders who are going to die!"

Chapter 4

"That's enough!" shouted Coach Truite, grabbing Jennifer's shoulders.

Jennifer sagged, and her crutches slipped away and clattered on the floor.

Seemingly out of nowhere, Rory appeared and caught Jennifer. He lifted her up easily, cradling her head gently against his shoulder. Her long dark hair fanned out over his arm, accentuating her waxen hue.

"Take her down to my room," ordered Coach Truite. "Marla, get her crutches. You — what's your name? Greg. Greg, get this wastebasket and all the mess out of here. We don't have any extra rooms, but I'll have maintenance in tomorrow to take care of everything. I presume that will be all right with you, Ms. Arlen? Or," the coach continued with sarcasm, "are you planning on seeing more ghosts?"

Mutely, red-faced, Delle shook her head.

"Good. See that it stays that way. I don't have time for troublemakers." Coach Truite looked around. "What are the rest of you standing here for?" she thundered. "Go to bed!"

The crowd hastily fell back and dispersed before Coach Truite, who stalked away without looking back.

Blushing, Delle looked at the dark-haired boy in the T-shirt and gray sweats who Coach Truite had ordered to help clean up the mess. Unconsciously, she tightened the sash of her bathrobe, then blushed harder.

He didn't seem to notice. He surveyed the mess with an appraising eye. Then he said, "There's a utility closet on the first floor. I'm gonna go get some cleaning stuff and we'll get this taken care of, okay?"

"Okay," said Delle. Her voice came out in a croak.

He looked up and his oddly flecked gray eyes met Delle's brown ones. He said, "Good. I'll be back in a minute. Don't play with any matches while I'm gone."

Delle didn't answer. She couldn't have, even if she'd been able to think of one. She felt as if someone had reached into her chest and given her heart a squeeze.

She didn't know how long she'd been standing there when a familiar voice said, "You can breathe now."

Delle jumped. Then her eyes focused and she realized that Mojo was standing in front of her, her wild hair even wilder, her eyes blazing with excitement.

"D'ja really see her? The Lady in Red? That is sooo cool. You are soooo lucky . . ."

"Are you serious?" said Delle. "I almost got killed!"

"Nah," said Mojo. "The smoke alarms were going off like crazy all over the building. Didn't you hear them? Thirty more seconds and the sprinkler system would have been on. I'll say one thing for our beloved coach. She's solid in an emergency.

"So, like, what happened an' all?"

Delle sank down wearily on the edge of her bed. "I don't know. One minute I was asleep and the next minute the room was filled with smoke and fire. But I was freezing. And I looked up and . . . *she* was standing there."

"How did you know it was *her*? I mean, you *are* talking about the Lady in Red, and not Coach Truite?"

"Very funny," said Delle. "I saw a woman. She had on a long red dress or skirt or coat of some sort. . . . I don't know. It happened so fast. One millisecond she was there, the next, gone. Vanished."

"And it was cold, you said." Mojo nodded wisely. "That's a classic manifestation of a ghostly presence. Bone-chilling cold." She opened her eyes wide. "The cold from beyond the grave."

"Mojo, please!"

"But why *you*?" Mojo went on, fingering the crystal at her throat. "Why should the ghost make a guest appearance where she'd never been seen before, just to torch you? Is she warning you specifically? Are you maybe fated to die in a fire, like she did?"

"Mojo!"

"Well, if it had been me, I would have — "

" — shouted for help like a sensible person?" asked a voice behind her and Greg came in holding a roll of paper towels, a bucket of soapy water, and a mop.

"No," said Mojo, apparently unaware of the special effects Greg was causing in Delle. "Well, yes, eventually. But I would have made a grab for her first. Asked her some of these very important questions."

Delle took the paper towels from Greg with nerveless fingers, tore some off, dipped them in the bucket of soapy water, and began to scrub at the smoke-smudged wall next to where the wastebasket had stood. Greg squeezed the mop out and began to mop up the fire extinguisher foam.

"Somehow, I don't think a ghost *or* a person dressed up like a ghost is going to stick around to answer questions. I mean, it's part of the whole ghost routine, right? My name is Greg, by the way. Greg Childs. You're Delle, I know by the name sign on your door."

"I'm Mojo," said Mojo. "Wow, Delle. The Lady in Red. Some people have all the luck."

The absurdity of Mojo's take on the whole situation suddenly made Delle want to laugh. There was definitely no one like Mojo back home in Cedar Bluffs.

Greg said, "Well, I'd ask the Red Lady why she needed to start a fire to get someone's attention. Seems to me a ghost would be attention-getting enough, all on its own."

Greg's comment stopped Mojo. "Hmmm," she said. Her hand went instinctively back up to the crystal around her neck. "Hmmm," she repeated, wandering out into the hall. She stopped and looked over her shoulder.

"I know something else I'd ask, 'cept maybe not from the ghost."

"What, Mojo?" said Delle in exasperated amusement.

"Why the girl next to you — one Ms. Susan

Worth, the name on her door says — slept through the whole thing . . ."

Mojo's voice trailed off as she drifted back down the hall.

Delle half-expected Greg to snort or make some patronizing comment about how weird Mojo was. She was surprised to find herself relieved when he didn't. Funny, she'd just met Mojo, but she really liked her.

Although not anywhere near the way she felt about Greg, Delle thought ruefully. Rory Hanahama might be cute, but he was nothing compared to Greg. *He* was making her heartbeat go ballistic.

Stealing a glance over at Greg she revised her opinion. Cute wasn't the word for it. It was as if he had a sort of dark magnetism in him. He wasn't tall and powerful like Rory. In fact, he was average in height, although clearly strong from the muscles she could see beneath his T-shirt.

"So what do you think?" said Greg, wringing out the mop a final time.

"W-what?" asked Delle, believing for a horrified moment that Greg had been reading her thoughts about him.

"What do you think about what Mojo said?"

Delle shrugged. "At least she believes me. I *wasn't* smoking, you know. And I did see someone dressed in red. But Jennifer's whole number about the cheerleaders being cursed . . ." Delle shuddered.

"You know the story of the Lady in Red?" asked Greg.

"Sort of. Mojo gave me the high points earlier this evening."

"The Lady in Red is, or was, a girl who was a student at the old Salem Girls' Normal School. That's what it was called. Anyway, she was a cheerleader. She was doing the cheerleader bit when the fire in the old gym broke out. In fact, the whole squad was practicing a really spectacular cheer using a hoop of fire. And she was goofing around and somehow it got out of control. . . . Everyone else escaped, but some people were badly burned, scarred for life. And she died. . . ."

Delle suddenly felt cold, ill. And terribly, terribly sad. "Poor girl," she whispered.

The two of them stood in silence for a moment. Then Greg said, "Don't take it so hard. It was a long, long time ago."

He took the towels and walked to the door. Turning, he surveyed the room. "It'll do," he said. "Maintenance can take care of the rest. Not too much damage, though. Looks like it was just one little piece of paper, maybe soaked in something to give it a quick, dramatic kick.

The metal trash can would've probably contained it."

"Thank you," said Delle.

"No problem," answered Greg. He smiled for the first time, a quick, hard smile. "For the record," he said, "I believe you, too. That you saw something, I mean. But I also agree with Mojo — why *did* the Lady in Red decide to visit you? Is she trying to *kill* you? Or *warn* you?

"Or maybe warn us all?"

The smile dying on her lips, Delle watched Greg go.

Again, it felt as if a hand had reached in and squeezed her heart. But it was a cold, cold hand this time. Cold as ice.

Cold as death.

Chapter 5

*When she screamed like that, it did something
to me.*
I liked it. It made me want to laugh.
It made me want to scream with laughter.
But I didn't.
Not yet.
Her screams are just the first.
She will not be the only one.
I like to hear them scream.

The second day of cheerleading tryouts
dawned hot and bright, hotter and brighter,
even, than the day before.

"At least the days are getting shorter now,"
offered Mojo, as she and Delle headed to the
gym in the humid early morning stillness with
a group of girls from Abbey House.

Funny, thought Delle wryly. Yesterday, I
didn't know anyone here. I was worried I was

going to spend my entire college career sitting in my room back at the Quad, talking to my roommate. Now suddenly, I have a whole new group of friends. I'm just catching on like wildfire. Amazing what a little notoriety can do for you.

Like wildfire. Like the nightmare last night that wasn't a nightmare at all. She didn't know how it had started, or where that cigarette had come from, but the fire had been real.

But had the ghost?

She looked at the girls around her, all of whom seemed to be waiting. Watching. Wondering the same thing.

Because of course, that was what it was. People were curious. Everyone had heard about what happened and if no one had had the nerve yet to ask Delle about the fire in her room and the Lady in Red, it was only because it was so early that no one really felt like talking. But if they survived this day's cheerleading workout, Delle was sure they would feel like talking soon.

Aloud, Delle said to Mojo, "Tell my body the days are getting shorter."

"Better yet, someone tell Coach Truite," a girl on the other side of Delle giggled. Undeterred by the fact that no one else seemed to be in the mood for conversation the girl said,

"I'm Joy Ferguson. How do you do?"

"Fine, thanks," said Delle automatically. "How are you?"

The girl giggled again and reached up to pat her silvery hair, which was woven into an elaborate French braid anchored by a bright orange ribbon. Had she gotten up early to achieve that perfect braid, Delle wondered. And why was she so cheerful at this hour of the morning?

Joy bubbled on. "I'm fine, thank you. Only I'm sore and I'm sorry to say it is *not* in all the right places."

"Wow," murmured Mojo.

"You're Delle Arlen, right? And you're Morgana Faye."

"Mojo," said Mojo.

"Right. I saw you last night."

Delle braced herself.

"In the lounge downstairs. And later on, after the fire and all." Joy giggled again. "Tell me, what was it like?"

"Scary," said Delle shortly.

Joy seemed surprised. "Scary? Really?"

"She *did* see a ghost," said Mojo. "Although *some* people wouldn't be afraid of a ghost, it's not that unusual that Delle would be scared by . . ."

"A ghost? Oh, that. I wasn't talking about the ghost! I was talking about that incredibly sexy boy. The one with the absolutely burning eyes who," Joy lowered her voice, "stayed in your room afterward. Greg. What was *he* like?"

For a stunned moment, no one said anything. Then on a burst of laughter, Delle gasped. "Him? Oh, he was fine. Just fine!"

The laughter spread, and the group swept into the old gym feeling at least a little light-hearted.

The feeling didn't last for long.

Coach Truite made sure this practice was even harder and longer than the day before.

"The basics," she kept telling them. "You're going to unlearn the bad habits you learned in high school. I want the straddle jumps crisp, the forward rolls tight. When you do a lift, you will hold form."

How many forward rolls can I do? thought Delle, as the day wore on. She was beginning to feel dizzy and sick. She looked up to find Marla standing there. Marla smiled sweetly.

"People learned a lot of bad habits at those little high schools, didn't they? Now, put both hands forward, flat on the ground. Go ahead, try it."

Gritting her teeth, Delle did another forward roll.

Marla cocked her head. "A little better. But keep praticing."

She moved to the next victim, leaving Delle seething.

"Smile," said a smooth voice.

"Rory! Is that video camera on?" Delle asked.

With the camera still against his eye, Rory said, "Yep. The truth about cheerleading."

Delle made a face and Rory laughed.

"No, seriously," he said. "Most of the footage is for training purposes, but I'm also going to do a cheerleading piece. I'm going to use it in my film class this year."

"Is this your dark side, your secret ambition?"

"Maybe," said Rory. "You can have a copy if you want. Dupes are easy to make. Just let me know."

"Thanks, but no thanks," said Delle.

Rory laughed again and moved away, still filming.

If the coach was a perfectionist and Marla was a sadist and Rory was a film director-to-be, Jennifer was endlessly patient, always ready to prompt people on words to the cheers and on the motions that went with them. When she reminded Delle to keep her palms up during one cheer, it didn't make Delle want to punch her out as it would have with Marla. She smiled at Jennifer in genuine gratitude.

"Thanks."

Jennifer answered, "Don't thank me. You're good, you know. That's probably why Marla's been picking on you. She's pretty insecure."

"Why?" asked Delle. "She's already on the team."

"Being a cheerleader is the most important thing in the world to Marla," said Jennifer. "It's like she doesn't have any other life. But if she had her way, she'd be the only cheerleader out there — at least the only female one."

"Not Coach's idea of teamwork," suggested Delle.

Jennifer shrugged. "Marla's the kind who's never satisfied. When she made the squad last year, she was furious that she wasn't elected captain, and she started trying to cause trouble among all the rest of us right away. Divide and conquer, I guess."

A strange expression passed over Jennifer's face. But before Delle could respond, Jennifer turned away to help someone else.

The long, hot, hard second day of tryouts practice dragged on. The only relief came right before lunch, when Coach Truite held cheerleading drills in the gym, dividing them into groups and working with one group at a time, allowing the other groups to rest.

But it seemed to Delle that, somehow, the coach still managed to single her out, that it was Delle's group that she kept out in the center of the gym the longest, and that it was Delle herself she criticized the most.

At last she waved them impatiently aside and motioned for the next group.

Mojo motioned for Delle to come join her where she was sitting crosslegged against the wall at the end of the gym, but Delle shook her head.

"It's cooler here," coaxed Mojo. "It's near the door."

Delle shook her head again and managed to croak, "Water."

"You shouldn't drink cold water right after you exercise," said Mojo. She stood up and walked over to peer anxiously at Delle. "I think it's bad for you."

"Yeah, right. Like I care," answered Delle crossly.

"But . . ." began Mojo.

Delle didn't hear the rest of Mojo's sentence. A horrible shriek suddenly filled Delle's ears. She jumped instinctively, grabbing Mojo's arm and making a dive for the open door of the gym.

"W-what the — " Mojo gasped just as someone else screamed, "Look out!"

The splintering crash of metal against wood

followed Delle, along with a crescendo of screams.

Delle looked back. For a moment nothing registered. Then she realized that had she gone over to join Mojo, or had Mojo not gotten up to join her, they would have been crushed beneath the old basketball backboard that had just torn loose from the gym wall and crashed to the floor below.

"I don't believe this," said Delle. "We could have been killed!"

Rubbing her arm, Mojo eyed Delle speculatively. "How did you know that was going to happen?" she asked quietly.

Delle's eyes fixed on the chaos that had ensued as Coach Truite forced everybody back from the destruction and gave various orders. Finally she realized Mojo had asked her a question. "Someone screamed," Delle answered.

In the middle of the gym, Jennifer stood motionless, staring up at the jagged places in the wall where the rusty old bolts had pulled loose. Then her gaze lowered to meet Delle's.

Why is she looking at me like that? wondered Delle.

"Are you listening? No one screamed. Not until we were already out the door," said Mojo.

Delle frowned, looked at Mojo. "What are you talking about?"

"We were already out the door when someone screamed, 'Look out' and that thing started to fall."

"Someone screamed," Delle said. "Didn't you hear it? It was . . . horrible."

Mojo eyed Delle a moment longer, then shrugged. "If you say so. But either you've got very, very bad luck or — considering what has happened to you these last few days — I'd say someone is out to get you."

Chapter 6

The rest of the afternoon passed uneventfully. Coach Truite drove them just as hard as ever. The only change in the schedule was that the rest of the practice that day was held outside while a maintenance crew cleared away the old backboard. They'd returned from lunch to find Coach Truite, hands on hips, berating the foreman of the maintenance and repair crew. "Disgraceful!" her words flew back to them. ". . . repairs at once . . . negligence . . . gross incompetence. . . ."

The words reassured Delle somehow. Although Mojo had said nothing more about what happened, Delle couldn't help but wonder. Was she jinxed? Was someone out to get her?

But why? She'd never made any enemies . . . unless you counted old weird Warren. And somehow, she didn't see him dressing up like a ghost or setting a wastebasket on fire or somehow causing an old backboard to fall.

She threw herself into the rest of the practice, determined to keep her mind off her terrifying brush with death. She also wanted to give the coach no opportunity to find fault.

She was only partially successful. As Delle lay gasping in the grass where she'd dropped on the final whistle signaling that the practice was over, Coach Truite, accompanied by Marla, paused to stare down at Delle. "I presume," said the coach, "that this practice — and your demonstrated lack of stamina — will convince you to forgo any further cigarettes."

"But — " Delle gasped.

"Good," said the coach, and strode away, slapping her clipboard against her thigh.

Delle fell back and moaned. It was so unfair. She didn't smoke. Never had. Never would.

But tell that to Coach Truite.

Sighing, Delle looked across the field. Scattered everywhere the cheerleader hopefuls lay, like the bodies of soldiers fallen in battle.

"You *are* unlucky, aren't you? I mean, last night's little cookout in your room, today's little accident in the gym. . . . No wonder Coach has really got it in for you," said Marla, a satisfied smile on her face.

"Thanks for sharing," said Delle sarcastically.

"My pleasure," said Marla.

"Go away, poison breath," said Mojo unexpectedly.

It was so totally out of left field that everyone was stunned into silence. Then Marla, her face a deepening crimson, sputtered, "You can't call me that. Do you know who I am?"

"A public nuisance, right at the moment," said Mojo.

Marla's mouth opened and closed like a fish's, but no sound came out. Then with an inarticulate gurgle, she turned and stormed off.

"Wow, Mojo, not bad," said Delle.

"Yeah," agreed Mojo in satisfaction.

"You shouldn't be smoking, you know. She's right," said a girl who had somehow managed to get through the practice without becoming totally drenched in sweat.

"You're Susan Worth," said Mojo suddenly.

The girl looked taken aback. "Correct," she said.

"Well," said Mojo, "if you hadn't stayed in your room last night while everything was goin' on, you'd know that Delle has already said she doesn't smoke. And I don't think she's a liar, do you?"

The girl flushed. "I was . . . I was asleep. I didn't hear about anything until this morning." She seemed to look everywhere but at Delle.

"I'm a heavy sleeper. But I *am* sorry about what happened to you."

"Thanks," said Delle.

A red-headed boy who had not spoken before said, bitterly, "Well, I don't believe you saw a ghost. I mean, isn't it fairly obvious? The Lady in Red, the fire, now this backboard falling in the gym. Someone wants to make this cheerleading team really badly. So badly, they'd even try to scare the rest of us away." His face contorted, then became a rigid mask. "Well, good luck to them. They're wasting their time on me. This is something I intend to *win!*"

With that, he, too, jumped to his feet and strode away through the late afternoon sun, as if he couldn't put enough distance between himself and the rest of them soon enough.

"Geez," complained Joy. "Everybody's so cranky. I'm just glad to be alive."

Is this girl for real? wondered Delle.

A voice spoke up. "You call this living? I think there's got to be more to it than this."

"Greg," said Delle without even having to turn around.

"Eyes in the back of her head. I like that in a woman," Greg said.

"Ugh. You make me sound like a flounder."

"At least you're not a *truite*," returned Greg.

"Huh?" said Joy.

"It's French for trout, Joy," Mojo explained. "Like our coach, old fishface."

"So," said Greg to Delle. "What do you think? Tonight — off-campus food. Off-campus fun . . ."

Before Delle could answer, Joy clapped her hands together. "It sounds wonderful! And so team-spirited. Everyone going out together."

Was that what Greg had in mind? Delle tilted her head back to look at him. He looked just as good from that angle. Although, thought Delle, possibly the way I look upside down might not be so special.

Greg smiled at Delle, then said to Joy, "We'll gather the troops in the lounge at Abbey House at — six-thirty? That gives everyone time to ease into something more comfortable."

"I'd like to ease into a new body," said Delle, without thinking.

This time, Greg's smile was even broader and Delle felt herself blushing furiously. Mojo's snort of laughter didn't help.

But before Delle could say anything else, Susan, getting to her feet, said seriously, "Just wait. I have a feeling we're all going to be hurting a lot worse before this is over."

Chapter 7

No one got hurt this time.
Too bad.
I would have liked that.
But I think they're beginning to be afraid.
If they're not, they should be.

Not everyone showed up, but Greg's sugges-
tion — or at least, Joy's interpretation of it —
had generated a good crowd, enough to practically take over Vinnie's, the funky pizza parlor on Pennsylvania Avenue. Marla had come,
of course, and Mojo and Joy and the angry red-
haired boy whose name, Delle had learned, was
Charles Pike.

And they'd all managed to really pump up
the volume in the place, giddy like kids out on
a field trip. Or prisoners out on parole, thought
Delle wryly. An easy camaraderie had settled
over the group as people ate pizza and moved

from table to table and got to know one another.

Joy had taken determined possession of Greg, at least for the moment, while Marla, to Delle's surprise, was talking intently to Charles. Rory had come late with Jennifer and the two of them now stood next to the counter, talking to an open-faced, easygoing-looking guy named Peter Nordstrom.

Something Jennifer said made Peter laugh, and the two bent their heads closer together. A moment later Rory, who'd been hovering protectively around Jennifer all evening, patted her arm and began to make his way across the room.

He sat down by Delle. "So, you're Delle, right? How're you doing?" he asked.

"I'm fine," Delle answered.

"You're doing better than I am, then." Rory smiled, turning the charm on high. "This week is turning out to be a lot more heavy-duty than I expected."

"Uh-huh," said Delle noncommittally. Beneath his charm, Delle sensed he wanted something. If it was more information about what had happened the night before, he would have to ask for it. Although the whole thing was becoming increasingly more dreamlike and unreal against the noisy, laughing, vivid reality of the pizza parlor.

He did ask. "So, Delle, what happened last night?"

Delle made a face. "Haven't you heard?"

"About as many versions as there are people in this room. But I'd like to hear it from you. I — I don't know. As co-captain, it just seems important to get the facts."

"Just the facts, ma'am," Delle couldn't help saying.

Rory nodded, smiling a little. "If you don't mind."

How could she mind? Briefly she told him what happened.

When she'd finished, Rory shook his head. "The Lady in Red, huh? You know, every year the school paper does a piece on her. One of those lighthearted, our-own-little-school-ghost, of-course-we-don't-really-believe-in-her stories. That's generally enough to head off any serious claims of 'sightings.' "

Delle asked, hesitantly, "You heard what Jennifer said? About last year? And the accident?"

"Yeah, I did. I have to say, it's not like Jennifer to give much credence to ghost stories. She's like me. Hardheaded. But she's been through a lot. An awful lot."

Delle nodded sympathetically.

Rory went on. "To be the only survivor of that bus accident . . . you ask yourself over and over, why? Why did it happen? Why me?"

"Well, what about you?" Delle asked.

"Me?" Rory said. He seemed startled by Delle's question.

"Yeah — how do *you* feel about being one of the lucky few?"

Rory paused, as if trying to decide what answer he should give Delle. Then he said, "Sure, I wonder, too. What if I hadn't gotten that other ride? But to be in Jennifer's place . . . she doesn't remember anything, you know. She remembers being at camp, she remembers packing to leave, she remembers giving her stuff to the bus driver to put in the luggage compartment . . . and that's it, until she woke up in the hospital."

"Oh, poor Jennifer," said Delle.

"Yes," said Rory. "Poor Jennifer. But maybe she's lucky she doesn't remember. Maybe it's best if she never does."

Delle felt the touch of that icy hand upon her heart. "Wh-what are you saying, Rory?"

Rory looked at her for a long moment, his expression enigmatic. Then he said, "Oh, you know. It was such a trauma. Maybe it's best if all those images of what happened stay buried in her subconscious somewhere. So she isn't, well, you know, *haunted* by them.

"So if Jennifer says anything to you about it all, especially about the Lady in Red, I think it's best not to encourage her, you know? It could make things worse."

"Oh," said Delle. "Sure." But she couldn't help wondering: Why was Rory trying so hard to protect Jennifer?

Was it genuine concern for her?

Or was it something darker? Like the fear that Jennifer would someday remember about the bus accident. Remember what had happened.

Remember that maybe it wasn't an *accident* after all.

Chapter 8

"Having a good time, Delia?" Marla said.

"Hi, Marla," said Rory, standing up. "*Are* you having a good time, *Delle*?" he asked, putting a special emphasis on her name.

Delle smiled. "Hello, Marla."

"Rory, I see you managed to dump Jennifer Doom on poor, unsuspecting Peter Nordstrom."

Rory's lips tightened, but he said, evenly, "I think Jennifer's been through enough without the co-captain of the cheerleaders ranking on her. Don't you, Marla?"

Marla had the grace to look momentarily embarrassed, but she recovered quickly. "We've all been through it, don't you think? And it *is* Jennifer who started the whole 'curse of the cheerleaders' thing. Can you explain that? I mean, since you and Jennifer are *so* close. So curiously close . . ."

"Drop it," Rory said.

Marla shrugged, then motioned with her hand to the boy next to her. "You remember Charles, Rory?"

Rory's charming, pleasant mask was back in place. "I can't say that I do. I'm sorry."

In contrast to Rory's smooth veneer, Charles's manner seemed abrupt and ungracious as he said, "No reason for you to. It's not like we were in the same crowd."

"Charles is a gymnast," interceded Marla. "And a very good one."

"I should have made the gym team, but it's not how good you are, it's who you know," Charles said vehemently.

"You'll make this team," said Marla. "With your talent, it'll be easy. I was noticing you today, and, believe me, I made sure Coach Truite was, too."

Delle said, "I didn't know the co-captains got to help *choose* the team. Do you?"

"No," said Rory.

"Yes," said Marla.

The two co-captains both stopped. Then Marla said, "Of course we don't choose. But we *are* assisting Coach."

"With the practices, Marla. Not the judging," said Rory.

Charles, who had been looking from one to

the other, said, "Well, it doesn't matter. I'm good. And this is one team I will make. Or . . ."

"Or what?" asked Rory, his pleasant expression belying the sudden menace of his tone.

Charles stopped. Then he shook his head in mute fury and turned away. Delle couldn't help but notice the peculiar grace of his movements, which contrasted so strongly with the rigidity of his manner — almost as if there were two people at war inside his body. She wrinkled her brow. It was funny, but for a moment, Charles had reminded her of her old boyfriend, Warren . . .

"Thanks, Rory," Marla hissed.

She was about to follow Charles, but Rory caught her arm. "I need to speak to you," he said. "Alone."

Marla looked down at Rory's hand on her arm and incredibly, for a millisecond, Delle saw Marla's face soften into a small, secretive smile. Then Marla looked up at Rory and said, furiously, "Take your hand off me!"

"If you'll excuse me," said Delle hastily. She slipped quickly away and looked around for Mojo and Greg. It wasn't curfew yet, but she was dog-tired.

Mojo was nowhere to be found.

Neither was Greg.

"Great," muttered Delle. "She's probably already beamed herself back to Abbey House."

As for Greg — well, she didn't like to think of the idea that he'd left with someone else.

Shaking that unpleasant thought, she patted her pocket to make sure she had the key to her room, then headed for the door.

It wasn't particularly dark. The days might be getting shorter, as Mojo said, but they weren't getting that much shorter. The blue darkness of early night had just fallen as Delle went out to Pennsylvania Avenue and began to walk back to campus. The joints all along the avenue were definitely jumping: people were coming and going, talking and laughing, filling the street and the air with a pleasing buzz of activity.

And she was part of it.

She smiled to herself, letting her eyes run idly over a gloomy, slightly gothic-looking house. Then her eyes focused on the neat Salem U sign out front:

NIGHTINGALE HALL.

Nightmare Hall. The smile slipped from Delle's face as she remembered Mojo's words. A lone light shone in one of the upper windows.

Delle shuddered, seeing against her will someone fashioning a noose, fastening it around her neck, stepping up onto a chair . . .

No. She turned away and picked up her pace. She couldn't think about that now.

A couple ahead of her turned and pushed into a burger joint. Music and laughter poured out and then stopped as the door swung shut behind them.

Turning onto campus, Delle strolled past the Quad, the all-girls dorm comprised of four large buildings enclosing a courtyard. Her room was on the second floor of one of the buildings. Even though the Quad had antiquated rules about boys and visitors and curfews, Delle liked living there. The people on her floor were a lot of fun, like Lacey Sakurada in Suite 2AB.

Delle was sure nothing terrible could ever happen in the Quad. Or at least, nothing more terrible than having to book it all night for an exam or put up with a roommate from hell.

Although Abbey House had certainly introduced her to some interesting people, too, she admitted wryly to herself.

She considered stopping by her room at the Quad and saying hello to her roommate, but she was too tired. Maybe tomorrow night, she decided. She passed the Student Center and headed across the Commons toward Abbey House. The blue velvet of the night deepened and the first stars began to shine.

The lights of Abbey House, in contrast to the one, lonely lit window at Nightingale Hall, gave off a friendly glow. Across Abbey Lawn, Peabody Gym made a darker outline against the sky.

Peabody Gym. Where some poor girl had died. So why had the ghost appeared at Abbey House?

Could a ghost haunt two places?

Did the Red Lady haunt the lawn in between?

Stop it, Delle scolded herself.

You don't believe in ghosts. You know — don't you — that it wasn't the Lady in Red at your door.

So if it wasn't, who was it?

At last she let her mind dwell on the fire last night and accident that morning, the incidents she'd been trying to forget all day.

Her thoughts flew instantly to Marla.

But why Marla? What did Marla have to gain by starting that fire or by pretending to be the Lady in Red? Or somehow managing to engineer the near disastrous accident in the gym?

No, that was just an accident. An unfortunate coincidence.

It was the fire that was the problem.

The fire and possibly Marla's involvement in it.

Was Marla some kind of psycho? It was entirely possible, considering her behavior, said a little voice inside Delle.

Stop it, she answered the voice. Just because you don't like someone — and they don't like you — doesn't mean they're a psycho.

Well, what about Susan? Susan, who had slept through the whole fire, or said she had. Maybe she'd been listening at the door the whole time, enjoying the trouble she stirred up, listening to Delle's desperate screams . . .

Would Susan do something like that? Set a fire and dress up like a ghost, then hide in her room, stripping off the red dress and hiding the evidence of her arson?

But why?

No reason. No reason at all, unless Susan was desperate to make cheerleader and considered Delle the main threat. Which wasn't likely.

Actually, the weirdest of the people she had met, Delle had to admit, was Mojo. But, Delle told herself before the little voice inside her could get started, just because someone was sort of unusual didn't mean she was a psychopath.

Oh, well, at least I know who it *wasn't*, thought Delle. It wasn't Jennifer. I would have noticed if the Lady in Red had been on crutches . . .

A sudden movement caught her eye.

Delle stopped abruptly. It wasn't possible! Or was it?

She saw it again.

The cold hand gripped her heart.

"No," she breathed. "It can't be."

But it was. A movement, the ghost of a movement: a faint, red, shimmering light passing from window to window, high in Peabody Gym.

Chapter 9

Delle looked wildly around.

But suddenly, the campus was very deserted. Very quiet.

And much darker.

I'm imagining things, she told herself.

The red light flickered from window to window. As if someone were pacing.

Or signaling.

But signaling who? Or what?

In spite of the warm, humid night air, Delle shivered.

She looked around again.

"Where did everybody go?" she whispered aloud.

Slowly she began to walk forward, keeping her eyes fixed on the flickering red light.

Could it be a fire?

She sniffed the air. No smell of smoke. And the red was so intense: not the dancing red and orange and yellow of flames. The light itself flickered, but it moved, slowly, evenly, from one window to the next.

Delle tried to picture the windows in her mind. It was an old-fashioned gym, with wooden bleachers that were folded up against the walls for the cheerleading workouts to give the maximum amount of space. Above the bleachers were the high, narrow windows covered with mesh to protect the glass. It would be impossible to get up to the top of the bleachers unless you had a ladder. Or unfolded a section of the bleachers.

Of course, Delle told herself, trying to kid herself out of the fear that was squeezing, squeezing at her heart: of course, if you were Mojo, you could levitate.

Which you could also do if you were a ghost.

I won't think about that now.

She rounded the corner of the dark building and looked back across the lawn. No one was walking across the lawn. No laughing couples. No security guards. No one.

Above the uncannily deserted campus, the lights of Abbey House shone serenely on. And in front of her, the old gym loomed, a vast, dark house of horror.

This is stupid, Delle thought. I should go get someone.

But who? And by the time she got back, whoever — or whatever — it was might be gone.

The gym was probably locked, she told herself. If it's locked, I'll go and get help.

The door opened easily beneath her hand, swinging noiselessly wide to pull her inside.

The darkness in the foyer to the gym was almost complete.

Where were the lights?

She fumbled for the switch and found it at last. It flicked as noiselessly as the door had opened.

And no light came on.

Almost as if she were in a dream, Delle crept forward, her hands out in front of her, groping in the faint light from the open door of the gym.

She was halfway across the foyer when the door gave a faint, protesting squeak — and swung soundlessly shut.

"Oh!" Delle gasped. She turned blindly.

But it was too late.

Now the darkness was complete.

And when she'd turned, she had lost her bearings. Where was she?

Where was she?

Trying to keep silent, to choke back the scream, trying to get her bearings as quickly as possible, Delle lurched forward.

Her hand touched something cold and wet.

"Ah!" But even as she stifled the scream in her throat, Delle's hand slipped down a familiar shape. One she had come to know well in the last couple of grueling days of workouts.

The fountain in the foyer by the gym door.

Running her hand across it, she reached out again.

Yes. The door. The door to the gym. Gaining courage by knowing where she was in the dense darkness, Delle slid her hand down to the door handle and pushed.

The door sighed open.

And Delle saw, high in the far corner of the gym, a figure in flowing robes that glowed red and horrible in the dark.

Slowly, slowly, the figure turned. Now Delle could see . . .

No, it wasn't possible.

But it was.

The thing was clothed in red from head to foot. A hood of red enveloped its head.

But there was no face beneath the hood.

Delle opened her mouth. Was she going to scream? Cry out for help?

She didn't know.

She never found out.

Because something grabbed her and then everything went dark.

Chapter 10

She was dying.

Gasping for air, trying to breathe, falling deeper and deeper into the darkness.

Into Death.

"Shhh," Death whispered in her ear. "Shhh. It's okay. It's me."

And she realized that it was not Death holding her against its chest. Death had no heartbeat, no warmth. Would not put its arm around her and stroke her hair soothingly.

"Okay?" came the whisper.

She nodded and the hand came away from her mouth.

In the darkness high above at the far end of the gym, the red light flickered and went out.

"Damn," said the voice, this time not bothering to whisper. "Stay here."

"Are you kidding?" she croaked. The figure who was not Death began to move away from her, where they'd been standing by the entrance to the gym. She caught his arm and stumbled after him through the darkness along the edge of the gym floor.

A minute later they stopped so suddenly that she thudded into him. She heard the flicking of switches.

The gym lights suddenly came on.

Delle saw that the stranger was Greg.

"What are you doing here?" she almost stuttered in her surprise.

He didn't answer. Instead he said, "Come on," and led the way across the gym floor to the far corner.

They both stopped and Delle followed Greg's gaze up to the top of the bleachers all neatly folded into place against the wall. It was there she had seen the light, and the eerie figure in red.

But no one was there now.

Delle looked for a ladder, a rope, any possible way that someone could have gotten up or down.

Nothing.

Then she became aware of Greg's arms around her.

She cleared her throat. "Ah, Greg? You never answered my question — what are you doing here?"

Greg, who'd been staring bleakly at the empty gym, looked down at her, his arms tightening.

"I followed you," he said simply.

"You *followed* me? What do you mean, you followed me?"

"I'd left Vinnie's. Stopped for a little while at the Student Center. Saw you pass and thought I'd catch up with you. Then I saw you veer off across the lawn toward the gym." He smiled reassuringly at her and after a moment, almost against her will, she smiled back.

So he hadn't gone home with someone else.

Then she remembered the ghost. "Did you see . . . did you see?"

Greg nodded. "Yep. Your Lady in Red. Did she look the same as last night?"

Delle frowned, remembering. "Y-yes. No. I'm not sure. It was all so fast . . ."

Greg shrugged as if it weren't important and, reaching out to catch her hand, began to walk back across the gym to the door. "What about you? Are you okay? I'm sorry if I scared you."

"I was already scared," confessed Delle.

"Were you? It was pretty brave of you to come in here, then."

Greg looked down at her admiringly. He smiled slightly.

She smiled back. Her heart was pounding, but this time it wasn't from fear.

"I'm not afraid now," she said softly.

"You're not?" He stopped smiling and reached out to flick the lights in the gym off again.

Then he kissed her. She'd never been kissed like that before. She liked it.

She kissed him back and sensed him smiling and laughed a little herself.

"So," said Greg, softly.

"So!" cried a harsh voice, and the lights of the gym flicked on again to reveal Coach Truite and Marla and Rory standing in the doorway.

Delle jumped, but Greg kept his arm around her.

He was so calm. How could he be so calm at a time like this?

"What seems to be the problem?" he said easily.

Her eyes snapping with fury, Coach Truite strode forward.

"*What* is the meaning of this?"

Don't tell them we saw the Lady in Red, Delle thought, trying to telegraph the warning to Greg with her eyes.

He wasn't looking at her.

"I should think it would be evident," said Greg coolly. Nothing more.

Marla snickered. Delle thought she saw a look of sympathy in Rory's eyes.

"Don't get smart with me! Tell me what you're doing here!"

"The door was open," said Greg, "so we stopped by on our way back to Abbey House."

Coach Truite's eyes narrowed. "The door was open?"

"Yes."

For once, Coach Truite appeared at a loss for words. Then she seemed to recognize Delle for the first time.

"*You!*" she said. "I suppose I should be grateful you're not in here smoking and burning *this* building down!"

"I don't smoke," cried Delle. "I keep telling you that!"

"Hmmph!" said Coach Truite. She paused, considering. Then she said, "Well, get back to the dorm. It's almost curfew. And don't let me catch you in here without my *express* permission again."

"Right," said Greg. He caught Delle's hand. "C'mon."

Coach Truite, Marla, and Rory watched in silence as the two left the gym. Delle resisted the impulse to look over her shoulder. She was sure she could feel their eyes on her.

"All very convenient," said Greg softly as they crossed the lawn.

"Yes," said Delle, thinking of Marla's nasty smile. "Wasn't it?" Then her thoughts took a quick spin and she said, "And now we can't even go back and try to find out if it was really a ghost."

"For the moment, anyway," agreed Greg.

"Do you think Marla set the whole thing up? You think that's how she was able to get Coach Truite there so fast?"

"Marla?" said Greg.

"Not Rory!" said Delle. "Rory wouldn't do something like that."

Greg flashed Delle a look. "Why not Rory?"

"Why would Rory, of all people, pull a stunt like that? What's he got to gain?"

"Why would Marla?"

That stopped Delle. After a moment, she said, "You're right. It just seems more her nature. But what would be the point of it?"

Greg shook his head. "What's the point of any of this?"

"The point is, *someone* is up to no good. I think it's someone who wants to scare the cheerleading team, to ruin the tryouts. That's why I didn't say anything about what we saw. Whoever it was, if we don't talk about what we saw tonight, is going to have to try something else, and soon."

"And maybe next time, we'll catch the 'Lady in Red,' whoever it is," Greg finished. "Sure. Why not?"

They'd reached the dorm. Greg stopped at the second floor landing. He looked up at the glaring overhead light, then back at Delle.

"I do my best kissing in the dark," he said. "See ya tomorrow."

He turned and walked down the stairs and was gone.

Chapter 11

Coach Truite lined them up in the middle of Peabody Gym. She surveyed them all sternly. Then she walked up and down their ranks, slapping her clipboard against her thigh. She was dressed from head to toe in black today, despite the steam heat that a morning of steady rain had created. All in black except for the silken orange embroidery on her sweatshirt: *Coach Truite.*

Everyone else was dressed in a hodgepodge of workout clothes, from baggy gray sweats to cropped shirts and shorts. And everyone else, except the coach, was drenched in sweat and breathing hard.

Some of the cheerleader hopefuls had been relieved to see the rain. Surely the downpour had meant that practice would not be as prolonged, as grueling.

Delle and Mojo had known better.

They had been right.

The practice had been the hardest one yet. And the day was only half over.

Back and forth along the lines of sweating, gasping students the coach paced.

Mojo muttered out of the side of her mouth, "All Coach needs is a riding crop and she'd look like something out of one of those old prison movies."

Delle bit her lip to keep from laughing. Or maybe to keep from crying.

"What I want from you is relatively simple. I want some indication that you are taking these tryouts seriously. Some indication that you want to represent Salem University as a cheerleader.

"But what I seem to be getting is whatever you people can spare from your nocturnal activities. From your incessant gossiping. From your *ridiculous* superstitions."

Delle felt her cheeks grow hot. Coach Truite was talking about her!

"You are here to try out for cheerleading positions that are open because of a tragic accident. An accident in which an outstanding coach and seven fine athletes lost their lives, and from which another has had to use every ounce of her courage and strength to recover."

Jennifer, who'd been sitting on a chair near

the gym entrance, suddenly seemed to shrink in her seat.

"To spread stories about a ghost and link it to the tragedy of this past summer is disrespectful, to say the least, of those who died.

"And I WILL NOT HAVE IT!"

Coach Truite roared the last words so loudly that everyone jumped and many people gasped.

"If I hear one more word about ghosts or anything of the sort, I will disqualify that person from the tryouts. Do I make myself clear?" Coach Truite's eyes swept the gym. For one brief, horrifying moment, they seemed to rest on Delle.

"Any questions?"

As usual, there were none.

Coach Truite nodded. "You are dismissed for lunch."

Delle watched in weary fascination as Mojo ate her way through a mountain of cafeteria food. "You're going to go up to do a herky jump and fall to earth like a rock," she predicted.

"Carbohydrate loading," mumbled Mojo around a mouthful of mashed potatoes.

Susan, whose own plate had been arranged, apparently, according to color, neatly finished off her salad and said, unexpectedly, "Carbohydrates and vegetables are the optimum training foods, you know, Delle." She began on her steamed broccoli.

"I know, I know," said Delle. She picked up a whole wheat roll and bit into it resignedly.

"I hate vegetables," said Joy. "Except carrots. And zucchini. And cucumbers. And bananas."

"Bananas aren't a vegetable," Susan told her.

"Whatever," said Joy, digging into some banana pudding.

"Speaking of bananas, what do you all think 'bout what Coach said?" asked Mojo.

Delle said, "I don't happen to believe in ghosts, but I didn't imagine what happened in my room." Or in the gym last night, she added silently.

"It doesn't make sense," objected Susan.

"What about that thing falling in the gym?" asked Joy.

"I believe you mean the basketball backboard," said Mojo. "And that was an accident. Wasn't it, Delle?"

She looked intently at Delle and Delle felt herself blushing. "How would I know?"

"You mean it wasn't an accident?" Susan asked. "That you think it was . . ."

"No, of course not! It was an accident. It had

nothing to do with what happened in my room. And nothing else has happened."

"No?" said Joy. "That's not what I heard." She looked around the table. "Are we supposed to be talking about this? Didn't Coach say we couldn't?"

"She has to catch us first," said Mojo.

Joy thought for a moment, wrinkling her brow and biting her lips. Then she said, "Oh." She looked at Delle. "That's not what I heard," she repeated. When Delle didn't respond, Joy prompted, "Last night?" and smiled slyly.

Delle hadn't told anyone about the Red Lady in the gym; so what was Joy talking about, she wondered. And why the big grin? Suddenly Delle realized that Marla had probably told everyone about Coach catching her and Greg in the gym the night before. "Oh. That." Delle shrugged.

But before Joy could pursue the subject any further, Mojo said, "Wow, look at the time! We'd better get going."

Delle flashed Mojo a look of gratitude and mouthed a silent "thanks." Then scooping up her tray, she fled from the table, her cheeks still burning.

That afternoon, the accident was real.
And no one knew quite how it happened.

Delle had been struggling, unsuccessfully, with a flip off the mini-tramp, securely rigged into a safety harness and spotted by Mojo and Peter.

"It's not working," she moaned in frustration, after spinning up and over, only to lose her place in the dizzy spin and end up dangling stupidly at the end of the harness.

Coach Truite strode over and grabbed Delle's legs. "No, no, no. Open your eyes. Marla, come here."

Seething and humiliated, Delle was forced to watch while Marla did a perfect flip off the mini-tramp.

"Good," said Coach Truite. "See? You have to keep your eyes *open*. Stay focused. If you don't, you will get hurt. And you'll endanger your teammates. Do it again." Without waiting for an answer, she strode away, barking at another hapless student who was attempting a back walkover.

"Good luck," sneered Marla, before turning to follow the coach.

"Here, let me give it a shot," said Peter. "You can take a rest."

"But what about what Coach said?" asked Mojo. "Delle, you should do it again."

Peter grinned. "Don't worry, Mojo."

Delle willingly changed places. As Peter put

on the harness, she took up her spotter position on one side of the mini-tramp.

Peter took a few tentative bounces, went up into a spin — and the harness came loose from its mooring on one side.

Delle and Mojo both lunged to catch him, but the uneven jerk of the harness had sent him spinning out of control. A millisecond later he came flying down with an ominous thud on the floor beside the mat.

"Peter!" gasped Mojo.

But Peter didn't answer. He lay there, white and still, his body at an ominous, unnatural angle.

"He's dead," Mojo screamed. "Peter is dead!"

Chapter 12

Of course he wasn't dead.
Too bad.
But it was still . . . delightful.
Delightful, the way the screams brought panic and fear.
Delightful, the way he lay there, not moving, scarcely seeming to breathe.
Delightful the horrible groans he made as they carried him to the ambulance.
They're beginning to be afraid now.
They suspect . . .
But they don't know. Not really.
They have no way of knowing that they are going to scream and scream and scream.
And then . . .

That night, Delle lay wearily in bed, staring at the shadows on the ceiling, her thoughts going around and around and around. Was there such a thing as a ghost? How could there be?

Thank goodness her instincts not to tell Coach Truite about what she and Greg had seen last night had been on target. She could just imagine what Coach Truite's reaction would have been.

Especially now.

I'm afraid, thought Delle. I'm afraid.

Because she knew, she *knew*, that what had happened to Peter could have happened to her. *Should* have happened to her.

And that it was no accident.

She played the scene back in her mind: Mojo, who after one harsh, frightened cry had looked at Delle almost accusingly before dropping to her knees besides Peter. Rory — with that damn video camera of his, the eye of it turned toward them all until Jennifer had grabbed his arm, her own low voice penetrating Delle's shocked senses: the Lady in Red . . .

And Marla, still as a stone, staring across the gym. Watching.

Waiting?

If it *was* a ghost, what was it trying to warn her about? This accident? Or was this one only the beginning?

Was the warning meant just for her? Or, as

Jennifer had insisted, was it a warning for all the cheerleading candidates?

Did the Lady in Red hate all cheerleaders because of the way she had died? Was her intent warning? Or *harm*?

Did she have something to do with Peter getting hurt?

None of it made sense.

Maybe someone just hates *me*, personally, thought Delle. But who? And why? I haven't been at Salem long enough to make any enemies, except Marla, who seems to hate everybody. And of course, she added wryly, Coach Truite. But Coach Truite wouldn't have to dress up like a ghost to convey her dislike to Delle. All Coach had to do was not choose Delle for the team.

So that left all the rest of the people trying out. And all the rest of Salem U.

It's my roommate at the Quad, thought Delle with a sudden flash of humor. She secretly hates me.

The thought of a psycho roommate made her smile momentarily because it was so ridiculous. But then her thoughts went back on the same treadmill.

It couldn't just be *me* that the ghost — or bogus ghost — is after.

So the most logical explanation, of course,

was that someone was trying to scare off the cheerleading competition. But if that was the case, that meant that it could be any one of the sixty-seven people trying out for junior varsity. And they had to scare the juice out of sixty-six other people.

It was a pretty big job even if you were really good at playing ghost.

But if that was the case, why did they start with me, wondered Delle. Was it just my bad luck?

Wait a minute. What if someone was trying to make it all look random, to disguise who the real victim was meant to be?

Or: victims.

The victims of the accident this summer.

Maybe the accident *hadn't* been an accident, like Marla had said. And maybe whoever it was had come back to finish the job. To kill off the rest of the original squad.

Or maybe one of the three people who'd survived had planned the accident and now meant to kill the other two survivors.

Yeah, right, Delle, she told herself. It was Jennifer. She engineered the accident, then threw herself out of the wreck.

Better yet, it was Rory, driving along the dark road behind the van, running it off the road and over the precipice . . .

Whoa. That actually could have happened. But why?

For that matter, Marla could have pretended to have the flu, then snuck out, driven back to the cheerleading camp, waited for the van, followed it, and . . .

This is crazy, Delle thought. I'm making myself crazy. And I'm going to feel horrible in the morning if I don't get some sleep.

She sighed and rolled over and punched the damp pillow. And finally managed to fall asleep.

When she awoke, the bed was rocking. No, not the bed. She wasn't in her bed.

Gingerly she sat up. Someone had dressed her. She was wearing a cheerleading outfit. Red and white.

And she was in some sort of vehicle. A car?

She sat perfectly still, fighting to maintain her composure.

Had she been kidnapped? Was this some kind of a joke?

What was going on?

"Hello?" said Delle to the darkness. "Hello? Is anybody there?"

No one answered.

But now her eyes were adjusting to the darkness. She seemed to be — yes, she was in some kind of van. Dimly, ahead, she could see the outline of someone driving.

Leaning toward the front seat, she tapped the driver on the shoulder.

"Who are you?" she asked. "What am I doing here?"

The driver accelerated without warning, ignoring her.

Angrily, Delle grabbed his shoulder.

She shook it hard.

"Answer me!" she demanded. "Answer me!"

With a jerk, the driver turned his head.

He looked at her with evil, dead eyes. Then he smiled triumphantly. "Dellllllll," he breathed.

It was Warren! Her old boyfriend, Warren!

"You!" Delle fell back. It couldn't be . . . it couldn't be . . .

Her hand touched something stiff and cold. Gasping, Delle spun around.

She wasn't alone in the van. She was surrounded by cheerleaders. Cheerleaders dressed in red-and-white uniforms. Cheerleaders clutching garish red-and-white pom-poms.

Cheerleaders who would never cheer again.

Dead cheerleaders.

"Noooooooo," Delle screamed.

And woke up.

* * *

She was shaking all over. She had never been so afraid in her life.

She'd never had such a vivid dream. It had seemed so real.

So real.

But it wasn't. It was just a dream. A nightmare.

Gradually, her heart slowed down to normal. Gradually, she relaxed.

It wasn't surprising she was having nightmares, given what she'd been through.

Forget it, she told herself. Get some sleep.

She closed her eyes.

She yawned.

And heard a soft tapping at her door.

And a voice breathing softly: "Dellll."

Chapter 13

"No!" gasped Delle. She sat up, clutching the covers.

"Delle, it's me, Greg. Open the door."

"Greg?"

"Shhhh!"

Hastily, Delle grabbed her bathrobe and went to the door. "Greg? What are you doing here? It's after curfew. If Coach Truite catches — "

"Get dressed. Wear dark clothes," said Greg. "Meet me downstairs by the side entrance. You can use the fire exit. I've jammed the alarm. And bring a flashlight."

"Who died and made you boss?" asked Delle, but Greg had already slipped away.

"Good grief," muttered Delle. She got dressed as quickly as she could and made her way downstairs and out the fire door, shutting it carefully behind her.

For a moment, she thought no one was there. Then, as silently as a shadow, Greg materialized at her side. In the dim exit light she saw that he was wearing a black shirt, black jeans and black sneakers.

"What's going on?" said Delle. "This better be good."

Greg seemed surprised. "We're going to the gym. Take a look around."

"I saw enough of that gym today to last me a lifetime," said Delle.

Greg's teeth flashed in a brief smile. "Yeah. But if whoever was there last night left any clues, they didn't have a chance to remove them. And I'm betting they didn't come back last night. Plus there've been a couple of 'accidents' I'd like to check into, wouldn't you?"

Delle returned Greg's smile slowly. "You're right. Let's go!" She caught Greg's hand and pulled him toward the side of the gym.

"Wait," said Greg. "Where are you going?"

"The long way around," explained Delle. "If we cut directly across the lawn, anybody could look out their window and see us."

"Good thinking," said Greg.

Keeping to the shadows and the shrubs, the two made their way at last to the gym entrance.

"It's going to be locked," said Delle.

"It's a pretty basic lock," said Greg. He

pulled a credit card from his pocket and bent over. Delle looked back over her shoulder.

The campus was the most deserted she'd ever seen it. How late was it? She hadn't looked at her clock. It had to be after midnight, at least.

She'd find out soon enough when the campus clock chimed.

Greg straightened. "Piece of cake." He pushed the door open and they slipped inside.

"Don't use your flashlight unless you absolutely have to," said Greg. "We'll wait till our eyes get used to the dark."

A few minutes later, they were making their way across the dark, echoing gym.

"Creepy," muttered Delle. "Even if I were a ghost, I wouldn't want to hang out here."

Greg stopped and switched on his flashlight. A tiny, pencil-thin beam appeared.

"*That's* your flashlight?"

He said, "The less light, the less chance someone will see us and catch us."

They started where the basketball backboard had pulled out of the wall. But maintenance had long since cleaned up every trace of the mishap. There was even fresh plaster covering the jagged holes where the bracing had torn loose.

"Zero here," said Delle.

In unspoken agreement, they moved toward the spotter harness, dangling from the center of the brace, pushed up against the wall with the mini-trampoline and the rest of the equipment.

They scrutinized the spotter harness brace.

But the broken rope was no longer there. It had been replaced by a clean new rope. In fact, both sides of the spotter brace rope had been replaced.

"These maintenance guys are *suspiciously* efficient," muttered Delle. "Come on." She headed for the far corner of the gym.

Carefully they examined the wall of pulled-up bleachers.

"Nothing," said Delle. "At least, nothing I can see."

"Yeah." Greg sounded disappointed. He craned his head back. "I wonder if there's a rope or something, maybe stashed up on the window ledge or something."

"Even if there is, how would whoever it was have gotten away? They would have had to come back down past us without us hearing them — and seeing them."

"True."

"Look, give me a boost. I think I can get enough of a toehold to get to the top and take a look."

"You sure?"

"Swap flashlights and gimme a boost!"

A moment later Delle was inching her way up the bleacher wall, barely able to get the tiniest toehold in the cracks. But at last she made it.

"You okay?" Greg's whisper floated eerily up through the dark.

"Yes."

Cupping her hand above the pencil flashlight, Delle examined the top of the bleachers. Nothing. Nor, as she crept along the line of windows, did she find a rope.

"Nothing," she whispered back down to Greg when she had finished.

"Nothing?"

"Nothing."

She lay full length along the top of the bleachers, and flicked the light around one more time.

And said, suddenly, excitedly, forgetting to be quiet, "Greg. I've got it!"

"Shhh! Got what?"

"There's like — like an old catwalk or something up here . . . and a sort of — trapdoor to the roof. If someone could have made it to the catwalk, they could have gotten out on the roof, no problem."

Greg's disembodied voice, after a pause,

said, "I think you *have* got it. But don't try it. Come on down."

"Don't worry," Delle whispered. "I'm a good athlete, but you'd have to be a super gymnast with nerves of steel to make that jump."

"Or crazy," suggested Greg.

"Or crazy," agreed Delle. A few minutes later, she slid down into Greg's arms.

"It's a start," said Greg. "I think we're onto something. Now, weren't we here before?"

"Yep." She lifted her face to his.

If Joy knew about this! she thought dreamily.

Suddenly she pulled free. "Did you hear that?"

They both froze. Then Greg said, "The gym door. Someone's got the key! Quick!"

Greg and Delle scrambled and slid across the gym floor.

"In here," hissed Greg.

A moment later they were in the boys' locker room.

And a moment after that, as they stood in the darkness listening, they heard the door into the gym open and the lights click on.

"Who's there?" Coach Truite's voice echoed hollowly around the gym.

"Geez," breathed Greg. "Doesn't she ever sleep?"

They heard the coach's brisk, heavy tread. Greg's hand tightened on Delle's.

The footsteps circled the gym. And stopped.

For what seemed like forever, silence filled the gym.

Only it wasn't silence. Delle could hear herself breathing. Could hear her heart pounding. Was sure she could hear even the trembling of her body.

Why couldn't the coach hear it too?

"Hmmph!" said the coach at last. They listened to her footsteps grow fainter and farther away. Then the lights went out and the doors shut and the key rasped in the lock.

They waited for a long, long time without moving, listening to the clock tower chime the fifteen minutes before the hour and then the hour.

Two A.M.

"I think we can go now," said Delle.

Carefully, quietly, they crept back across the gym. Carefully, quietly, they made their way back to Abbey House.

Delle half expected to find the emergency entrance locked up tight. But it wasn't.

She turned to Greg.

"Wow," she said. "I thought I was gonna die tonight."

"You did?"

"Yeah." She grinned. "Next time we go out, we have to go some place besides the boys' locker room. It really stinks. You guys are pigs!"

Before Greg could answer, she reached up and kissed him, hard. "See you in a couple of hours."

Then she slipped in the door and ran lightly up the stairs to her room.

Chapter 14

Mojo and Delle sat on the wall at the Student Center looking out over the Commons.

"Two more days," said Mojo. "Tonight, tomorrow night, and then, tryouts." She bent her head over her palm and studied it.

"Trying to tell yourself your fortune?" teased Delle.

Mojo made a face. "You can't read your own palm."

"Oh." Delle reached over and grabbed Mojo's hand. "Long life. Enormous wealth. Oh, yes, and you will be chosen for the junior varsity."

Pulling her hand back, Mojo shook her head. "You shouldn't make fun of it."

"You don't *really* believe that stuff, do you Mojo?"

"You think I'd lie about it?"

"No! It's just — I mean, everybody knows

that — " Delle floundered, then concluded lamely, "that it's not real."

"Maybe not to you," said Mojo. "But to me it is. I believe in a lot of things. Fate. Destiny. Luck. Karma. Ghosts."

Looking at Mojo's intent face, Delle realized Mojo wasn't kidding. And for a moment, she felt uneasy.

"Have you always believed in all that stuff?" Delle asked.

"Yes," said Mojo simply.

"You don't believe in voodoo, do you? You know, dolls and hexes and all that stuff?" The conversation was making Delle even more uneasy.

Mojo stared at Delle for a moment, then grinned unexpectedly. "Nah. Even I have my limits, Delle."

"Good," said Delle, relieved. She looked out across the Commons. The hot weather had begun to slack off at last. So, apparently, had the ghost. No one had gotten hurt since Peter's fall, and he was recovering rapidly from two cracked ribs and a concussion.

Delle had begun to relax a little, to enjoy herself.

Even if I don't make cheerleader, she thought, I'm already having a great time.

She looked over at Mojo, who had her eyes

closed and her head thrown back as if she were meditating, and smiled. Although she'd only known Mojo a little while, Delle felt as if she'd known her forever. Whatever else happened at these tryouts, there was that.

And then, too, of course, there was Greg.

Not even Coach Truite's disapproving eye or Marla's snide remarks could take that away.

I feel good, thought Delle. Everything is going to be all right.

Delle unlocked the door to her room still in the same great mood. But before she could go inside, Susan's door flew open and Susan backed out as if she'd been shot from a cannon, to slam bonelessly against the hall wall.

"Susan?" asked Delle.

Susan's face was dead white. Her lips moved soundlessly.

"Susan?"

A tremor went through Susan's body.

"Susan!" Delle grabbed Susan's shoulder and gave her a little shake. "Susan!"

Slowly Susan seemed to focus.

"D-Delle?"

"Are you okay? What's going on?"

"I — she — it. In my room." Delle was astonished. She'd never seen Susan anything but icily calm, even in the face of Coach Truite's most withering criticism.

But now Susan was like another person. A crazy person.

"Your room?" asked Delle. "What's the problem?"

She turned and Susan uttered a stifled moan. "Be careful. Oh, my God, be careful."

Cautiously, Delle pushed the door to Susan's room open. For a moment, nothing registered except the extreme neatness of the whole narrow space. Which in a way made what lay on Susan's bed all the more horrifying.

It was a doll.

A doll dressed in a little cheerleader's uniform. Red and white.

The red of blood, splashed on the pillow, where the doll's head had been grotesquely severed from its body.

And next to the doll, a bloody piece of paper, crudely lettered.

Go. Fight. Win.

DIE.

Chapter 15

Not even Susan's warning had prepared Delle for what she'd seen. Nausea surged in her throat. Carefully, gingerly, as if in a nightmare, she backed out of Susan's room.

And turned wordlessly to face her.

Susan, keeping her voice steady with an obvious effort, said, "I just got home. And it was there. My door was locked. I don't know how it got there."

"I don't believe this," said Delle. "I'll go get Coach."

"NO! No. You can't do that! It'll ruin my chances to make the team. You heard what Coach said. You know she wouldn't even let me try out if she found out about this!"

"But — "

"Unless that's what you want! Is it? Is it, Delle?"

"Susan, chill, okay? No, it's not what I want.

But what are we going to do? I don't want to touch that — that thing."

Some of the color was returning to Susan's face. "Mojo. She's cool, right?"

"Yeah. Like ice. Maybe Mojo is a good idea. I'll go get her."

Mojo answered the door the moment Delle knocked.

Almost as if she knew I was coming, thought Delle. Casually, aloud, she said, "Expecting someone?"

Mojo grinned. "Maybe I had a feeling you were coming."

"Mojo, this is *serious*."

"What? What happened?"

"Come on. I'll show you."

Delle and Mojo hurried back down the hall. Susan was still standing there, but she was no longer pressed against the wall, and the blank, terrified look had left her face.

"What is it?" asked Mojo.

Susan nodded. "In there."

Delle pushed the door open and ushered Mojo in, watching her face. She didn't know what to expect. Certainly not what Mojo did.

She backed up so fast, she almost knocked Delle over. The two of them tumbled out into the hall.

Mojo turned to Delle. "What is this! Your idea of a bad joke?"

"No way!" said Delle.

"Sure!" Mojo was practically shouting. "Sure. Making fun of me, that's what it is, isn't it!"

"Shhh! Mojo, stop it."

"People are looking," said Susan in an agonized undertone.

It was true. A couple of girls had already stuck their heads out of their dorm rooms.

Delle managed a weak smile in their general direction and then practically shoved Mojo into her room. Susan followed and shut the door behind her.

Mojo's face was bright red. "I can't believe you'd *do* something like this. I just can't believe it!"

"I didn't! Mojo, will you *listen*?"

"I thought you were my friend!"

"Please!" pleaded Susan.

Something in Susan's voice seemed to reach Mojo.

She took a deep breath. Waited. Took another deep breath and folded her arms.

"Okay. I'm listening."

"It's not a joke," said Susan desperately.

"It isn't, Mojo. I swear it," Delle added.

Mojo looked from Susan to Delle. Then she

unfolded her arms and said, slowly, "What's goin' on?"

Quickly Susan and Delle explained what had happened. As she listened, Mojo's eyes grew veiled. When they'd finished, she said, "So what d'ya want me to do about it?"

Susan said, "Get rid of it?"

"What? *Me?* Why me?"

"Please," urged Susan.

"Ugh," said Mojo. She heaved a deep sigh. "Okay, I'll do it . . . but you have to come with me."

"Mojo, no," Susan pleaded.

"That's the deal. All for one and one for all. The three of us are in this one together."

"Fine. Let's just get it over with," said Delle.

Mojo looked at Susan. Slowly Susan nodded.

"Come on, then."

Mojo led the way back to Susan's room. She stopped at the door. Looked back at Delle and Susan. Pushed the door open.

For a moment, the three girls stood staring. Staring at the red-smeared pillowcase.

But there was no note. No doll.

They were gone.

Chapter 16

"I don't believe this," said Mojo in a hushed tone of voice for about the hundredth time.

It was after midnight. After curfew. But Susan, Mojo, and Delle still sat in an uneasy vigil in Susan's room. The red-smeared sheets were bundled in the laundry basket in the closet. They'd stuffed a towel under the door and drawn the blinds so no one could see the light was on.

The little room felt close and warm and stifling.

Delle felt like she was suffocating. "It happened," she said aloud to Mojo. "Believe it."

"This is heavy duty stuff," said Mojo. "I mean, someone is out to get someone big time."

"But it doesn't make any sense," Susan said. Apart from the fact that she resolutely refused to look in the direction of her closet, she had regained her outward composure. "Why leave the doll in the first place, if you're just going to take it back later?"

"To shake us up," said Mojo. "I mean, think about it. Not only did someone get into your locked room somehow, but they watched the whole scene, saw us go into Delle's room and then walked right in and took the doll and the note back. It yanks *my* chain, believe me."

She paused, then looked at Delle. "Delle? What's the matter?"

But Delle didn't hear her. She was suddenly seeing Greg, crouched in front of the Peabody Gym door in the dark, working open the lock. Hearing his voice saying, "Piece of cake." Remembering how casually he had told her he had jammed the alarm on the fire exit door in Abbey House. And how he'd just happened to be there at the gym that first night . . . and how he was the one who'd cleaned up the evidence of the fire . . .

"Delle?"

"What? Oh." Hastily Delle replayed Mojo's last sentence in her head. "Yeah. It yanks my chain, too."

It wasn't possible. It couldn't be Greg.

Could it?

"What do we do now?" asked Susan. "We're agreed, everybody understands that, right? We can't tell Coach Truite."

Mojo shook her head in emphatic agreement. "Def not. Coach would take all three of us out. Remember that little speech she gave?"

"Who could forget it?" said Delle mechanically. *It couldn't be Greg. It just couldn't!*

"You really don't think this warning was meant just for me?" asked Susan. "You think it was meant, for, well, everybody?"

"Yeah, I do," said Mojo. "But, like, you didn't react the way they wanted . . ."

"The way *I* reacted the other night," pointed out Delle. "You know, big screams, big crowd scene."

Susan looked at Delle solemnly. "I believe I would have reacted the same way, had my room been on fire."

"Thanks, Susan," said Delle.

"Anyway," Mojo went on, "this fruit loop, whoever it is, wanted to scare you — and wanted you to do the job of scaring everyone else in the dorm. But you didn't. And among the three of us we — what's the phrase I want — yeah, we contained the situation. So like, nobody knows.

"Except us. And believe me, I'm pretty shaken up." But Mojo's eyes sparkled. Clearly, she was excited as well.

In a way, thought Delle, Mojo and Greg were

alike. He obviously enjoyed living dangerously, too.

Hmmm.

"Do you think that note meant what it said?" Susan pressed on. "You know. The part about us . . . about us . . ."

"Dying? I don't know," said Mojo. "Look at what happened to Peter."

"It's probably someone who wants to be a cheerleader so bad, they'd do almost anything to make us scared," Delle said. "But probably not *kill* somebody. It's probably just a fright trip," she added quickly, seeing the fear on Susan's face.

"So what do we do?" asked Susan again.

Delle looked grimly at her two friends. "We keep our eyes open and we wait," said Delle. "For whatever happens next."

Waiting, as Delle was soon to discover, was as bad as anything that had happened before.

Walking wearily across the lawn the next morning, she found herself studying the others covertly, trying to read guilt on their faces. If someone yawned, she caught herself wondering if it was because they'd stayed up all night planning their next move. Or maybe suffering from a guilty conscience.

It was hard to concentrate. When Greg or

Charles or Rory threw her up into the air for a cheer and caught her around the waist with strong, sure hands, Delle wondered if those were the same hands that had twisted the doll's head from its body. The same hands that had maybe, maybe tampered that summer with the bus that had gone so inexplicably out of control and killed the junior varsity team.

Because in spite of what Delle and Susan and Mojo had agreed on, Delle wasn't sure she believed it was some rival, desperate to make the team.

She kept thinking that it had to be more than that. Because Susan and Mojo didn't know about the Lady in Red at the gym. Only she and Greg knew about that.

Unless the Lady in Red had been Mojo. Or Susan.

It was like some bad old movie, the tough private eye saying, "I trust no one. I suspect everyone."

Everyone.

Jennifer crossed Delle's line of vision, awkward on her crutches.

Everyone, Delle told herself firmly. Even Jennifer. Because maybe Jennifer was the one who'd started it all. Maybe Jennifer *had* sabotaged the van.

Maybe that's why she was still alive. So miraculously alive.

And maybe now she was just waiting for the chance to finish the job with Marla and Rory. And maybe the other things were just a snow job, to throw them off track. Especially Jennifer's outburst that first night, when she'd insisted that the Lady in Red had come back to warn them all of their doom.

Or maybe it was Rory. Rory, who was so protective of Jennifer. Maybe he was just waiting for her memory of the accident to return. And then when it did, he'd be right there to quiet Jennifer's memories forever.

Or Marla. Maybe the reason Marla was so mean was that she was *crazy* mean. Really, really crazy.

Or maybe Rory and Jennifer together had . . .

Stop it, stop it, stop it, Delle told herself. She couldn't stand it anymore.

She didn't want to think about it anymore.

But then, she didn't want to die waiting, either.

Chapter 17

Now they're getting it.
Getting it good.
I thought she was going to die when she saw that doll.
I like to hear them scream.
I want to see them die.
Dead cheerleaders.
Scream, team. . . .

Coach Truite walked up and down the lines of first- and second-year students, surveying their perspiring faces, dishevelled hair, the T-shirts and shorts that clung damply to their bodies, listening to the panting and gasping for air that they tried to conceal as she passed by. She slapped her clipboard rhythmically against her thigh as she walked.

Delle kept her face expressionless as the coach passed.

The last day of practice and the horrible words on the note hadn't come true. Unless you counted being worked to death doing cheers as a life-threatening situation.

Coach Truite finished her tour and went back to the front and turned to face her troops.

And Delle's mouth dropped open in shock.

Coach Truite was smiling. A nice, normal smile!

Although Delle couldn't say she *liked* the coach, now that the week was over, she had come to respect her. All the cheerleader hopefuls had improved so much, thanks to Coach Truite.

Still smiling, still slapping the clipboard against her thigh, Coach Truite said, "As you know, tryouts are tomorrow afternoon in Peabody Gym at one P.M. I want you to know that I think the judges — who have presided at many cheerleading tryouts here over the years — will have as difficult a job as they have ever had. I want to congratulate each and every one of you. These practices have been as grueling and difficult as I knew how to make them. And every single one of you has given it your all. I would be proud to have all of you be a part of my cheerleading squad. And no matter what happens tomorrow, you are all winners.

"That is all."

Coach Truite turned and walked briskly away. When her red- and white-clad figure disappeared into the gym, all of them broke ranks in unholy glee.

"Allllright!" cried Joy, spinning out into a series of cartwheels, two-, one-, and no-handed. Mojo bent effortlessly into a series of backflips. Delle found herself screaming and laughing and spinning around and around with Susan and Greg and, amazingly, Marla.

"We did it, we did it," screamed Susan. "We survived cheerleader boot camp!"

"Smile for the camera," Rory said, and the cheerleaders-to-be and not-to-be obliged him with a rowdy, raucous cheer.

Pandemonium reigned, and only when they realized that passersby had begun to gather and stare did they settle down and begin to break up into groups and head back to Abbey House.

"Wasn't that nice of Coach Truite?" gushed Joy.

"Practically human," agreed Mojo.

Charles, walking nearby, said sourly, "I bet it's some kind of a trick."

Even Marla looked taken aback by that. "No," she said. "I think she was pretty sincere."

Like you'd know, thought Delle. But she kept her thoughts to herself. She felt too good to get in anybody's face.

"I'm going back to the dorm and take the world's longest bath and then I'm going to take the world's longest nap — until, like, noon tomorrow," announced Susan. "I *was* going to organize everything for moving back over to Lester Dorm, but . . ."

"Hey, live dangerously," Mojo finished for her.

Susan smiled. She had definitely loosened up in the last couple of days, decided Delle. Something about being companions in danger, maybe. *Live dangerously.*

But nothing had happened since they'd found the doll and it had disappeared.

For a little while, she'd almost forgotten.

She looked up and, somehow not unexpectedly, met Greg's eyes.

He hadn't forgotten, she was sure. Nor had he seemed surprised when she'd told him about the doll. He'd just nodded, slowly, thoughtfully.

The exhilaration drained out of Delle, leaving her feeling tired. So tired.

Because this peace was bogus. False. It couldn't last.

Something else was going to happen.

Go. Fight. Win. *Die*.
Something terrible.
And soon.

"Why so glum, chum?" asked Mojo cheerfully. "Have some carbos."

Delle, who was sitting propped against the closed door of Mojo's closet later that night, took the slice of pizza automatically from Mojo's hand.

Somehow, Mojo's room had become the designated party room that night, and half of Abbey House was crammed inside it or hanging around in the hallway, eating pizza and drinking soda.

"Euuuw, garlic," said Joy.

"It'll keep away the vampires," someone said.

But will it keep away the Lady in Red, wondered Delle. She glanced warily at the door, almost expecting an apparition to appear in answer to her thoughts.

But all she saw was Jennifer and Rory, deep in conversation. Jennifer kept looking past Rory, her face impassive.

Who was Jennifer looking at?

Delle leaned forward, craning her neck. Marla?

Delle had had enough of Marla these past

few days. Too bad she was the co-captain. It was a cinch that she'd do everything she could to make everybody who made the scream team miserable in the coming year.

Too bad the Lady in Red hadn't taken Marla out.

Jennifer shook her head, glanced once more at Marla, then shook her head again. A fleeting expression of anger crossed Rory's face and he clamped his hand down on Jennifer's arm.

She looked down at his hand, then back up at him and something in her expression made Rory withdraw his hand hastily.

What are they talking about, wondered Delle. What are the two survivors saying about the third? What's wrong with this picture?

It made Delle uncomfortable.

"Smile," suggested a voice in her ear.

"Forget it," she answered, without looking at Greg. Then, striving for a lighter tone she said, "So, where have you been?"

"Around," said Greg.

Delle made a face, her eyes still on Jennifer and Rory.

Suddenly, Rory's face grew stormy and he spun around and disappeared from sight.

"Trouble in paradise," observed Greg unemotionally.

"Hardly paradise," Delle said, shifting her

gaze to Greg's impassive face. What does Greg know that he isn't telling me, she wondered.

And then Marla was there, her hand like a claw on Delle's arm. "How's our little bad luck charm doing?" she cooed.

For a moment, Delle was too surprised to speak. Then, in the silence that had fallen among the three of them, she realized that Greg had remained as impassive, as distant, as before.

Why doesn't he say something, Delle wondered.

But he kept silent. Waiting. Watching.

Delle jerked her arm free. "I wasn't around when all the cheerleaders were killed this summer, Marla," she snapped before she could stop herself. "*You* were."

She turned and walked away.

Delle caught up with Susan, who was walking slowly down the hall to her room. As she walked, Susan kept looking over her shoulder.

"What are you doing?" asked Delle, in exasperation. "You're giving me the creeps."

"I keep waiting for Coach to jump out of nowhere and shout, 'It's past curfew!' "

"Is that all?" asked Delle.

"I'd rather have Coach jumping out than . . . ," Susan lowered her voice, "whoever left that doll."

Delle said, slowly, "I'm sure it was just someone's sick way of trying to scare you so you won't do well in tryouts."

"But why me?" protested Susan.

Delle looked at her in surprise. "Because you're good."

The compliment made Susan flush. "I am?"

"Can't you tell? I think you're sure to make the team."

Susan flushed even more. "You do?"

"Yep."

"Oh . . . thanks. Listen, Delle, will you wait while I check my room? You know, just in case . . . ?"

"Sure," Delle said with more assurance than she felt.

Susan reached in her pocket and pulled out her keys. She fumbled with the lock, her hands shaking.

The keys slipped from her hand and fell to the floor.

"O-oh," gasped Susan. She bent and snatched up the keys. Looked back at Delle and then past her down the hall.

Delle fought back an impulse to turn and look, too.

At last Susan turned back to the door. Got the key in the lock. Reached gingerly inside and flipped on the light.

Unconsciously, Delle took a deep breath.

Susan pushed the door open.

No one was inside. Nothing was waiting for Susan.

Not tonight.

"Whew," said Delle.

"Yeah," said Susan.

Did she sound — disappointed? Couldn't be, thought Delle.

"Well, see ya tomorrow, Susan."

" 'Night, Delle."

At the door of her own room, Delle paused and, with unusual clumsiness, fumbled with her own key.

My hands are *not* shaking, she told herself firmly. And *nothing* is waiting for me on the other side of this door.

But what if there was? If nothing was in Susan's room, maybe something — or someone — was waiting in her own.

The key turned in the lock.

Delle gave the door a tentative push.

It didn't move.

She frowned.

She pushed the door hard — and almost fell into the darkened room.

With a smothered cry she scrambled to her feet, scrabbling for the light.

At last it clicked on.

She turned, half-flinching . . .

Nothing.

Maybe I was wrong, thought Delle. Maybe everything that is going to happen has already happened.

Putting all thoughts of what *had* happened out of her mind, Delle got into bed. If I let this get to me, if I let this affect my performance tomorrow, she lectured herself, then whoever is doing all this will have won.

Go to sleep, she told herself sternly.

And somehow, eventually, she did.

Footsteps woke her.

Footsteps, soft as breath, passing over her head.

She awoke instantly, her eyes open wide, staring up into the dark.

Footsteps.

But not in her room. Her tense muscles relaxed fractionally. Until she realized that the footsteps were coming from the floor above. The third floor of Abbey House.

The empty floor that was never used. That was closed up.

The floor where no footsteps were supposed to be.

It must be someone having a post-curfew date, she thought and closed her eyes again.

But they wouldn't stay closed. Against her will, she found herself staring up once again into the dark.

Faint footsteps. Almost inaudible.

Except that the night was so still. And dark.

They moved haltingly, with no rhythm or purpose.

Did ghosts make sounds when they walked?

With that thought, Delle sat up and grabbed her bathrobe. A moment later she had slipped out into the hall and was gliding toward the fire stairs.

For a moment on the landing, she hesitated. Should she go get someone? Maybe wake Susan up? Or Mojo? Or even Greg?

But whoever was upstairs might be gone by then. And if it was just someone meeting someone else, she didn't want to be a snitch.

And that's probably all it was. Probably Charles and Marla, she thought, making a face. The perfect couple.

The red EXIT light cast the stairs in a lurid glow as she climbed up them. Suddenly she realized that she'd forgotten her flashlight.

But the lights upstairs were bound to work, if she needed them. And once her eyes adjusted to the darkness, she wouldn't need a flashlight anyway. It wasn't *that* dark, she told herself.

She half expected the door to the third floor

to be locked. But it wasn't. It yielded easily beneath her hand.

"Great," she muttered, remembering what had happened at Peabody Gym four nights before. "Déjà vu."

She pushed the door open slowly and stepped into the third floor hall.

It was completely still and dark. A faint musty smell assailed her nostrils. Clearly the floor had not been used for a long time.

She waited in the dark, nerves tense, as her eyes adjusted. Soon vaguely familiar shapes began to swim up out of the night: the darker outlines of doors, the bump of the water fountain.

It all should have been reassuring. But it wasn't.

Delle squared her shoulders. She stepped forward.

In the distant reaches of the hall, something moved.

Delle froze, straining to see. To hear.

But everything became still and silent again.

This is ridiculous, she thought. She edged forward, trying to step softly so that she wouldn't wake up anyone below. "Hello," she called in a hoarse whisper. "Hello, who's there?"

The movement was more pronounced this

time. Almost as if something were writhing in the dark. Something trapped. Or in pain.

The icy fingers of fear touched Delle's heart, tapping a frozen counterpoint to its hot, frightened pounding. She suddenly wished, more than anything on earth, that she had not come to the third floor. Suddenly would have given anything for a flashlight. Suddenly realized that maybe, after all, she *did* believe in ghosts.

And she suddenly believed, as she had never believed anything in her life, that someone — or something — was behind her.

With a great effort of will, she turned her head.

Chapter 18

No one was there.

She was alone.

Except for whatever was waiting for her at the end of the hall. *I'm tired of being afraid,* thought Delle. Almost angrily, she stepped forward. She took a deep breath and said loudly, firmly, "Who's there?"

For a second her voice hung suspended in the dark silence of the hall.

Then, without warning, a blinding flash of light scalded Delle's eyes. With an involuntary cry of terror she threw up her hands.

The light went out. Unable to see, Delle lurched forward, groping for something, anything solid and real and safe.

Instead, iron hands gripped her wrists and she was spun around. She stumbled and crashed against a wall, her head slamming against it.

She slid to the floor as unconsciousness began to creep over her. A red haze filled her eyes.

Above her a voice whispered harshly, "Before I'm through, you'll be glad to die . . .."

Someone began to laugh.

And then Delle knew no more.

"Delle?"

Delle groaned and turned her head away from the light. It made her temples throb.

Where was she? Why did her head hurt so badly?

"Delle?"

The light. She remembered a blinding flash of light. Feebly she struck out at the light she could see now between her half-opened eyes.

"Delle . . ."

"Susan?" murmured Delle.

"Are you okay? What happened?"

Delle struggled to sit up against the wall. She raised her hand to her head. She could feel the beginnings of a killer lump.

Great, she thought.

"I don't know," she said to Susan. "I heard something and came up here to see what it was and I — "

A long, drawn-out groan froze both girls.

"W-what was that?" whispered Susan.

Again the sound came, hollow and agonized.

"You don't think it's the ghost, do you?" Susan snatched up the flashlight and pulled on Delle's hand. "Let's get out of here!"

"No, wait."

The sound came again. Reaching out, Delle took the flashlight from Susan's hand and shined it down the hall. At the outermost reach of the beam, something lay on the floor.

No, not something. Someone.

"Help me, help me get up," ordered Delle. She staggered to her feet and braced herself against the wall, waiting for the dizziness to pass. Then she said, "Come on."

"Delle . . ." said Susan hesitantly. "Maybe we should go for help."

"Good grief, Susan! You came up here to see about me without going for help! What are you afraid of now?" Without waiting for an answer Delle walked purposefully down the hall.

And stopped. "Oh, my God," she breathed.

Sprawled on the floor was Jennifer Li, her crutch viciously snapped and scattered in pieces around her. A thin line of blood glistened beside Jennifer's head.

"She's dead," Susan's voice rose hysterically.

"Shhh!" Delle bent over Jennifer, who had stirred and murmured something. "Jennifer?

Can you hear me? It's me, Delle."

Jennifer murmured inarticulately, then slowly opened her eyes. For a moment, she stared at Delle blankly. Then with a little cry she reached up and grabbed Delle's arm.

"Don't hurt me!" she said. "Please don't hurt me!"

"Go get help," Delle said over her shoulder to Susan.

"No! No, I'm fine." Awkwardly, Jennifer sat up. She put her hand to the side of her head and moaned. When she pulled her hand away, it was sticky with blood.

"Ohhh," breathed Susan.

"Susan. Calm down. Now." Delle turned the flashlight on Jennifer. "It's okay, Jennifer. It looks like one of your earrings got torn out of your ear. And you've got a nasty bruise just behind your ear."

Jennifer swallowed hard, then said, "It doesn't matter." She caught sight of a mangled piece of crutch lying at her feet and moaned softly.

But she said, "I'm fine. Let's get out of here. Okay?"

"What's going on?" asked Susan plaintively.

"I'll tell you everything. But first let's get out of here. Now. *Before she comes back.*"

* * *

"Before she comes back," Delle repeated. "What did you mean by that, Jennifer?"

The three girls were sitting in Jennifer's room, just as Susan, Mojo, and Delle had sat earlier that week in Susan's room, pondering the terror that seemed to be stalking them all.

Except that Jennifer didn't seem to be particularly terrified. Studying herself now intently in the mirror, and making faces, Jennifer deftly put the finishing touches on bandaging her earlobe.

"I wonder if I'll have to get stitches," she said. "Oh, well. One thing spending most of your summer in the hospital gets you used to, it's stuff like this."

Susan shuddered, but Delle said, "Who did this to you?"

"It's a good thing I have more than one crutch, isn't it?" said Jennifer. "After all, they don't come in left and right and now that I only need one, I can just use the other one." She twisted the top back on the bottle of peroxide, pressed the cloth against the bruise, and turned to face Susan and Delle, smiling brightly.

"*Jennifer*," said Delle. "Will you quit with the perky cheerleader routine and tell us what happened?"

For a moment longer, Jennifer's smile

stayed in place. Then, suddenly, Jennifer leaned forward and buried her face in her hands.

"Oh, God, oh, God," she moaned. "I don't know. I don't even know where to begin."

"What were you doing up there?" asked Delle.

Jennifer lifted her face from her hands to study Delle intently. At last she said, "I — I got a note. I thought it was from Rory. It said for me to meet him up there at midnight. He said it was important. We'd . . . had a fight. I thought it was about that."

Delle suddenly remembered what had happened between Jennifer and Rory outside Mojo's room earlier that evening. But all she said was, "Go on."

"When I got up there, he wasn't there. I thought I should probably wait. I was coming back down the hall when. . . ."

"What?" Delle wanted to scream with impatience. She ground her teeth together and winced at the warning throb the now walnut-sized lump on the back of her head gave.

"I saw her . . . she came out of nowhere. Suddenly she was standing there in front of me. I — I turned to try to get away. I thought I'd made it but somehow my crutch slipped . . .

something hit me in the head and that's all I remember."

"The Lady in Red," breathed Susan. "Was it her?"

Jennifer nodded and winced as if the movement made her head hurt. "Yes," she said softly.

The three of them sat quietly for a moment. Then Delle said, "Jennifer, are you sure?"

Jennifer met Delle's eyes. "You think I'm imagining it, don't you? But you saw her, too!"

"I saw someone who could have been dressed like the Lady in Red," said Delle.

"Really? Then where did she go so fast that night when the fire started in your room? No one else saw her. Except you."

Susan said, "Delle, what happened to you up there?"

"I heard footsteps overhead. I knew the third floor was closed off and I thought I'd go check it out." Delle shrugged. "Before I could, someone checked me out."

"It's a warning," Jennifer insisted. "The Lady in Red always appears before something awful happens. And now she's been seen twice. Something terrible is about to happen. Something even worse . . ." Jennifer's face contorted into a mask of pain and terror, ". . . even worse than what happened this summer."

Chapter 19

I'll never sleep again, thought Delle. She rolled over, punched her pillow, rolled back over.

Susan was back in her room, Jennifer was safely in hers.

Safely?

Were they sleeping? wondered Delle. Or were they lying there in the dark, waiting for ghosts, afraid of nightmares, trying to understand what had happened?

Trying to imagine what was going to happen?

Delle sighed and sat up, pulling her blanket around her shoulders. I'll never sleep again, she thought. At least not in this dorm.

Accepting that the next few hours would be spent awake, watching, waiting, somehow made it easier.

Whoever heard of pulling an all-nighter before cheerleading tryouts?

Slowly, carefully, she tried to organized her thoughts. Tried to make some sense out of the bewildering, terrifying events of the past few days.

First there was the fire in her room. And the figure, whoever it was, standing in the door.

A breath of air came through the open window of the room. It felt cool and welcome against Delle's cheeks. Unlike that other night when the air had been so warm, smelling of cut grass . . .

Delle's eyes widened in the dark — her windows!

Her windows had been open that night. She remembered that now. And someone had closed them.

But who? Had it been whoever had set the fire? Had they come through the windows?

The windows. Delle frowned, searching for an elusive thread of reasoning, of explanation. But it wouldn't come.

She put it aside and moved on to the next incident: the backboard falling. That could have been an accident. The gym was old and not in the greatest shape.

Or it could easily have been deliberate. Something to cause a little chaos. Or possibly a serious injury.

Anybody could have done that.

No help there.

But the next accident, when Peter had been hurt, was no accident. Delle was almost certain of that. She couldn't believe the safety equipment wasn't kept up-to-date.

But whoever had done it had somehow gotten rid of any evidence of tampering. Or at least, she and Greg hadn't been able to find any.

And it wasn't necessarily directed at her.

Delle frowned, remembering the sequence of events: Marla had demonstrated the flip. Mojo had been spotting.

Jennifer had been there earlier, helping Susan with the maneuver.

Rory had been all over the gym with that stupid video camera of his.

Had the accident been intended for her?

Or was it just another random bit of terrorizing by whoever was stalking the cheerleaders?

Stalking me, thought Delle.

Resolutely she shook the image off, and concentrated on the night she'd seen the ghost in the gym.

That would have been easy to fake. And it wasn't necessarily aimed at her. Anybody could have been drawn in.

After all, Greg had been, too.

Or had he? Greg, who was so quick to pick a lock.

Like the lock on her dormitory door the night the fire was set and the cigarette butt was planted?

No.

What reason would Greg have to do something like that? Unless, beneath his dangerous charm was something truly dangerous. Someone truly crazy . . .

She remembered his expression earlier that night during her confrontation with Marla. Watching. Waiting. Detached. Almost inhuman.

Wasn't that how psychopaths worked? Terribly charming.

Terribly dangerous because they were so charming?

No.

No, no, no.

Pulling her thoughts back from that path, Delle moved on. The doll. Someone had done that to Susan. Someone must have wanted to threaten the whole team.

And had almost succeeded. If she and Mojo and even Susan had been less calm, less levelheaded, everybody would have known about the doll and the threat. So why take the doll away afterward?

To make Susan look hysterical, overimaginative? To cause Susan to doubt her own perceptions?

Shaking her head, Delle sighed. It didn't make sense.

Any more than luring Jennifer up to the third floor hall had made sense. Except that whoever it was had wanted to frighten Jennifer. Maybe even kill her.

Or had they?

Delle suddenly flashed on the deft way Jennifer had bandaged her earlobe. Was it possible that Jennifer — or even Jennifer and Rory — had set that up? That Jennifer's hysterical outbursts about the Lady in Red were just an act? That Jennifer was trying to . . .

To what?

Delle groaned and yawned and rubbed her eyes. The first faint edges of gray dawn had begun to push the dark away. A bird had begun to sing, tentatively at first, and then more confidently as others took up the chorus.

The long night vigil was over, but she was no nearer to any answers. Except one.

Before I'm through you'll be glad to die, the voice had whispered.

Someone hated the cheerleaders — the ones

trying out, the ones already on the squad — enough to threaten them. To frighten them. To hurt them.

And maybe to kill them.

It was such a lovely game, so full of chills and thrills and screams. And pain. And blood.
Too bad it had to end.
Too bad it would have to end so soon.
But the ending would be the bloodiest, most painful, most fun part of it all . . .

"Hey wake up! How can you sleep at a time like this!"

Delle started up out of a deep, mercifully dreamless sleep. "Uggh ar?" she mumbled.

Mojo's voice on the other side of her room door said, "Delllle!"

"Justaminute," mumbled Delle, rubbing her eyes and stumbling toward the door. She was stiff and sore — no doubt from sleeping sitting propped up — and her head ached from not falling asleep until the safe light of day.

Delle opened the door and Mojo bounded in.

"Are you ready to go?" asked Mojo, sketching a motion with her hands. It was the first line of one of the cheers.

"I dunno," said Delle, trying to smile.

Mojo rolled her eyes. "The correct response is, 'That's what you know!' "

"Yeah, yeah," said Delle. She surveyed Mojo. "You look great!"

"Thanks," said Mojo. "You, I hate to say, don't look so hot."

"Had trouble sleeping," said Delle. For some reason, she was reluctant to tell Mojo all that had happened.

"Nerves?" said Mojo. She cocked her head. "That doesn't seem like you."

"Hmmm," Delle answered noncommittally. "Geez, look at the time! I've gotta hustle."

"Listen, meet me in my room in fifteen and we'll go grab something to eat. Doughnuts. Coffee."

"How can you eat at a time like this?" teased Delle.

"I can *always* eat," said Mojo. "Besides, you'll need the carbos."

"Okay," said Delle. Then she added, "But I'm not eating any doughnuts!"

"Breakfast of champion cheerleaders," Mojo retorted as she slid out of the room.

Apparently they weren't the only ones intent on carbo loading, or just getting some last-minute moral support. The cafeteria at the Student Center, normally deserted on a Saturday, was full of polished, pulled-together, cheerful cheerleader hopefuls.

"Ugh," said Mojo, stopping inside the door. "Doesn't all this perkiness just make you wanna throw up?"

Delle laughed, and for a moment felt better. "It is pretty intense," she agreed. She allowed Mojo to lead the way through the line and to a table off to one side of the sea of bright color and hyper chatter.

Not everyone had come, she noticed, picking at her dry toast while Mojo began taking random bites out of what seemed an obscene number of various kinds of doughnuts heaped on her plate. Marla, for example, was nowhere to be seen. Nor, unsurprisingly, was Susan or Jennifer.

But Rory was there, at the head of a large table of people. He exuded a calming sort of confidence and authority.

Following Delle's gaze, Mojo said stickily, "He's got i'made, huh?" She licked the jelly off her fingers and elaborated. "I mean, he's already on the team."

"True. But I think it's great he's here."

"Takes that captain stuff pretty seriously, doncha think?" asked Mojo.

"Well, somebody has to, and it's clear Marla doesn't. It's just a status symbol to her."

Mojo grinned. "Yeah. Like I don't think Marla would've been our fearless coach's first choice for the team."

Delle grinned back. "Me, either."

Mojo plunged happily into random gossip about the other cheerleader hopefuls, but Delle's thoughts stayed on Rory.

He did take his responsibility seriously. Maybe too seriously? Maybe behind all that charm was some kind of weirdo. Someone who got a charge out of scaring the very cheerleaders-to-be he'd be captaining. Maybe someone who liked a threatening situation because then he could step in and be a hero.

Suppose . . .

Suppose Rory felt guilty somehow about the accident that had killed his teammates. Responsible, even though he wasn't. Would that be enough to push him to some kind of extreme? Some kind of terrifying extreme?

Hard to believe. Much easier to believe of Marla. Except that when you got down to it, Marla was too simple. Too simply mean. Haunting dorms and gyms in the dead of night was not her style. For one thing, it would interfere with her beauty sleep.

". . . about that time."

Mojo was looking at her watch and Delle realized that everyone, as if by some prearranged signal, was gathering up their things and getting ready to head toward the gym.

A heap of half-eaten doughnuts lay on Mojo's plate. Eyeing it, Delle said, "You're going to go up to do a stag jump and come down like a dead deer."

"Ha!" said Mojo. "Just wait and see."

It's almost time.
Tick tock.
Knock knock.
A little cheer.
A lot of fear.
It's almost time for you all to die. . . .

Chapter 20

The next few hours passed like a dream. Looking back, Delle never could decide whether it was a good dream or a bad one.

Although all the people trying out got there early, the gym was already filling up. Clearly the junior varsity tryouts were a social event at Salem, at least this year. The whole feel of the tryouts quickly took on a surrealistic circus aspect. Someone had festooned the gym in red-and-white bunting and Salem U banners. The bleachers had been let completely down on both sides and a sea of faces looked down toward the gym floor. Delle and Mojo and everyone else were directed to the last set of bleachers in the corner of the gym by the locker rooms. Farther down, in the center behind a long table, were the judges.

Although Delle was used to crowds and noise and competition, she suddenly felt overwhelmed. It was too much. Too much . . .

Something terrible was going to happen.

The sudden shrill of a whistle startled Delle. It was exactly one o'clock and Coach Truite, in black slacks and a red-and-white-striped shirt, stood in the center of the floor. Such was the force of her personality that the swell of noise and talk gradually subsided until everyone was watching her silently.

She nodded, as if she expected no less.

In the expectant hush, she introduced the judges and the two co-captains, who, "while not voting judges, will be allowed to offer input into the decision."

Marla smirked. Rory remained impassive, serious.

Mojo made a rude noise.

Coach Truite explained the procedure: groups of six would do required cheers. There would be two preliminary rounds, with people eliminated on each one. Then would come the final round from which the few lucky winners would be selected.

"Six new cheerleaders and two alternates will be chosen," Coach Truite concluded. "They will be formally introduced to the school tonight at the memorial service here at Peabody at eight.

"Good luck to everyone."

The tryouts began.

Delle watched everything as if it were in super slow motion. When her turn came to join her group in the first set of cheers, Mojo had to poke her in the back to get her attention.

"Go on!" hissed Mojo. "I mean, be relaxed, but not in a coma, okay?"

Scrambling to her feet, Delle leaped after her group, taking her place at the end of the line:

> "Two bits
> Four bits,
> Six bits
> A dollar
> All for Salem
> Stand up and holler!"

She leaped into the air, pumping her fist, enjoying the crowd's reaction. It was an easy crowd, a willing participant. She smiled at the sea of faces and, coming down into the next cheer, began to feel better.

Nothing was going to happen. How could it, in this crowded gym in broad daylight?

> "S-A-L-E-M!
> Who's going to win?
> Salem!

Louder!
Salem!
Louder!
SALEM!"

Forward flip, drop into a split. Not everyone could do that and even those who could, couldn't do it as smoothly as she could.

She raised both arms and increased the wattage of her smile and saw one of the judges, a stern-looking man, smile back marginally before making a note on the tablet in front of him.

After that, everything went from super slomo to high speed. She was burning up. It was if the night before had never happened, as if the whole terrible, long ordeal of tryout week had never happened.

When the first-round eliminations were made, Delle knew she'd made the cut before they even announced it.

The second round went even better. As she finished her required cheer, Rory, sitting behind the judges table, caught her eye and gave her a quick, approving nod.

Yes.

Yes. She'd almost forgotten she was a winner. Was used to being a winner. Had almost forgotten that she could hold an audience in the palm of her hand, could control a crowd, wooing it, settling it down, pumping it up.

Owning it.

She was almost sorry when the second round ended.

Now they sat, sixteen of them, on the bleachers, taking a breather while the judges conferred and the crowd muttered and pointed. It was still an easy crowd, but a mysterious alchemy had taken place over the last grueling two hours: now the crowd had favorites and while it didn't boo those who were not in favor, the polite level of some of the applause was almost as deadly.

Deadly. Delle put the thought out of her mind. She wouldn't think about trouble, about danger now.

The only danger she would acknowledge would be the danger of not making the team. The danger of not concentrating and so screwing up.

She looked down the line: Mojo, Susan, Joy, Greg, Charles . . . Charles wasn't much of a crowd favorite, in spite of the range and grace of his motions. Maybe it was because his smile looked fiercely practiced instead of real somehow. Joy, however, had the crowd eating out of her hand. How did she manage, Delle wondered, to flirt with an entire gym full of people, all at once? It was definitely a gift, a gift as useful in cheerleading tryouts as all the herky jumps and look-Ma-no-hands back flips Charles could muster.

Coach Truite stood up. The crowd knew what to do this time. It had gotten quiet before she even reached the center of the gym.

The finals.

They seemed to go by in a flash.

Delle gave it everything she had. Would it be enough? Suddenly she wanted it more than she had ever wanted anything in her life. She caught Mojo's eyes and Mojo gave her a thumbs up. Then they sat, like kids outside the principal's office, waiting for the judges to tally their scores.

"Uh-oh," whispered Mojo.

They watched as Marla leaned forward and said something. Rory seemed surprised and shook his head. The judges had all turned and were listening.

The argument seemed to grow in intensity. Several times, Marla looked toward the bench.

Delle felt as if Marla were staring directly at her. Was it possible?

Would Marla be able to keep Delle off the team?

The argument continued. Then, suddenly, with an impatient shake of her head, Coach Truite turned back to the table. Marla sat slowly down, a frown of discontent on her face.

The decision-making process seemed to go on forever, but at last Coach Truite stood up. She didn't look at the crowd, or over at the bench. She kept her eyes fixed firmly on the piece of paper in her hand. Without introduction or comment she said, "The new junior varsity squad is as follows:

Morgana Faye.

Greg Childs.

Joy Ferguson.

Paul Mori.

Delle Arlen.

John DeLucca.

The alternates are:

Susan Worth.

Charles Pike."

"We did it, we did it!" Mojo screamed in Delle's ear. Then the crowd was upon them.

Pandemonium reigned. People who hadn't won smiled bravely and said congratulations. People who had won were polite, trying not to seem *too* triumphant. Coach Truite joined in the melee, pausing to shake each person's hand. Her congratulations to Delle were brief, but surprisingly cordial. "You did a good job," Coach Truite told Delle. "You deserve it."

"Thanks," gasped Delle in surprise as Coach Truite moved away.

"*Some* people deserved it," said another, far less cordial voice. Marla Pines put her hand possessively on Charles's arm and stared meaningfully at Delle.

Delle lifted her chin. "Congratulations, Charles. I look forward to being on the squad with *you*."

Charles looked startled, then confused as Marla began to sputter and Delle turned away. "I'm the captain," Marla said behind her, "You can't talk to me like that."

"I wasn't talking to you," said Delle, moving through the sea of bodies.

At the edge of the crowd, by the gym door, she found herself face-to-face with Jennifer. Shifting awkwardly on her spare crutch, Jennifer held out her hand.

"Congratulations, Delle," she said. "You won."

"Yes," Delle answered. "Thank you."

The two girls stood silently. Then Jennifer said, in a low, urgent voice, so softly Delle almost didn't hear her: "Be careful."

"What do you mean, Jennifer?" Delle asked just as softly, just as urgently. "Do you know something you haven't told me?"

But Jennifer didn't answer that. She only said, before turning clumsily away, "Winning isn't everything. *Staying alive is.*"

Chapter 21

Abbey House was empty now. Everyone, the winners and the losers, had cleared out to go to their respective dorms. Cheerleader boot camp was over.

"Now," said Mojo, irreverant to the end, as they lugged their suitcases back across campus to the Quad, "the real torture begins. You know, Delle, it's a good thing we're not in the same dorms at the Quad. I have a feeling the squad is going to be spending *a lot* of time together."

"But it'll be quality time," laughed Delle.

"Yeah, right," Mojo retorted. "Listen, let's meet here at Quad Main later and go over to the gym for the memorial ceremony together."

"Done deal," agreed Delle.

"See ya later," said Mojo.

"See you," agreed Delle.

Delle dragged her suitcase up to her room.

Her roommate wasn't there, but that was okay. She looked around the nice, clean, ordinary, unhaunted room with a sense of relief. No place like home, she thought.

With her suitcase unpacked at last, Delle flopped down on the bed in exhaustion. When she'd first made cheerleader, a thousand years ago back in high school, she thought she'd made a quick trip to heaven. Now she'd made cheerleader again. She'd gone from being a cheerleading captain in a small town to part of the junior varsity of a big university.

What next, she thought. Everything will be okay now, won't it?

What could happen now?

Was the Lady in Red satisfied? Or was this just the beginning? Would more people be hurt?

Delle groaned softly. Anything could happen. At practice. At a game. Going to away games on the bus . . .

Yes, she'd made cheerleader in the big leagues now.

And possibly gone from cheerleader heaven to cheerleader hell.

"Looks like some party," said Greg, falling into step beside Delle and Mojo.

Ahead of them, Peabody Gym glowed like a

jack-o-lantern in the dark, and couples and groups of people were drifting toward it from the parking lot and from the campus.

A couple stopped in front of them and waited beneath the glow of a sidewalk lamp.

"Hey, Joy," said Mojo. "Hey, Paul."

Joy giggled. Then she said, as if she were in the middle of some conversation with them all, "It makes me feel funny, though, you know? I mean being presented as the new cheerleaders and all? And to have a memorial for the ones who, who . . ."

"Died," said Greg abruptly.

"Yeah." Joy nodded.

"I'm sure they'll be extremely tactful about it," said Mojo in a voice that said *NOT*.

"Well anyway," said Joy. "We made it. *We're* the cheerleaders now."

"Yeah, team," muttered Greg. "C'mon."

Although they were right on time, the gym was already almost packed to capacity. But Coach Truite caught sight of them and motioned them to a section of bleachers in the far back corner of the gym, where Marla and Rory and Charles and Susan were sitting. Jennifer, Delle noticed, was sitting there, too, slightly off to one side, her expression unreadable.

Surveying the seats, which were not by any means the best in the gym, Greg observed,

"See? The privileges of being cheerleaders are already upon us."

Delle looked back over her shoulder at the crowd still pushing through the doors of the gym and a sudden sense of unease filled her.

"Greg," she whispered softly, urgently.

But Greg didn't hear her.

The noise was deafening.

Now the last of the crowd was being directed to seats. The gym was filled to bursting.

I can't breathe, thought Delle. *I've got to get out of here.*

But it was too late. Too late.

Smiling, nodding, she sat down between Greg and Mojo.

Couldn't they feel it? Couldn't they feel that something was terribly, terribly wrong?

Mojo and Greg began cracking jokes.

Marla turned her shoulder to them, and leaned against Charles.

Jennifer stayed where she was, huddled miserably on the bleachers, staring down almost as if she were in a trance.

Delle leaned across Mojo and said, "Jennifer?"

Jennifer didn't move.

"Jennifer?"

No answer.

Delle thought, Jennifer looks like a deer,

trapped in the headlights of an oncoming car.

An official-looking man stood up and approached the podium. Ah, yes, Dean Rhodes, the assistant dean of the school.

"I guess the dean was too busy," said Mojo. "Or maybe she doesn't like cheerleaders."

Dean Rhodes cleared his throat and began his speech.

The panic rolled over Delle in waves, drowning waves. She couldn't hear his voice. He droned on and on. Phrases and words swirled through her mind and disappeared: fine young people. . . . the best and the brightest. . . . those who died so tragically, Kathy Butler, Louise Veniero, Sally Ann Smathers, Reginald Trout, David Carlson. . . . the goals of all fine athletes everywhere . . . winners who never quit . . .

And all the while her senses screamed *Danger, danger, danger.*

But she could only watch his lips move, could only sit, frozen, as the memorial plaque was unveiled and the solemn ritual of dedication and remembrance was concluded.

Could only sit and wait.

Trapped.

Two bits, four bits, six bits, a scream.

Someone's going to kill this team.

Too.

Too late.

"Delle?"

For the second time that day, Mojo had to prod Delle to her feet. With a feeble smile of thanks, Delle stood up woodenly and followed the rest of her new team down onto the floor.

Coach Truite began to speak.

Delle stared at her lips.

What was she saying?

But nothing came through.

So Delle smiled when the others smiled. Stepped forward and shook hands when they did.

Stepped to one side while Dean Rhodes took the microphone for closing remarks.

A vast lethargy crept over Delle. She wanted to yawn, to lie down somewhere and sleep forever.

Sleep. She would be safe if only she could sleep.

Beside her, Mojo tensed.

"Smell that?" she muttered.

"Hmmm?" said Delle.

"Smoke," Mojo said.

Chapter 22

"And in conclusion," said Dean Rhodes.

"Smoke!" said Mojo, loudly and clearly this time.

"Fire!" someone in the crowd suddenly screamed.

Dean Rhodes turned, his mouth dropping open.

"Fire, fire, fire!" Others took up the cry.

It was like the fire in her room, thought Delle, staring at the black curls of smoke inching up the far side of the gym. Only this time it was much, much bigger. Much, much worse.

"Everyone remain in theirs seats . . . please be calm . . ." Dean Rhodes pleaded.

But those nearest the exit doors had already begun to push forward.

The screams grew louder. The smoke grew thicker.

"The doors are locked!" someone cried. The

crowd surged against the doors now, a churning sea of terrified people. They raised their fists and banged on the door. Pressed against the doors with all the weight of the crowd.

The screams of terror became mixed with screams of pain.

And the doors held.

"Oh, my God, oh my God, oh my God," a voice chanted mindlessly and Delle realized it was Susan, out of her mind with fear.

"Stop it," she said. "Stop it!"

Panic was about to overtake them all. "Stop it!" Delle yelled. She stepped forward. Clapped her hands. Made them into a megaphone for her mouth.

"SALEM U, SALEM U!

THIS IS WHAT WE'RE GOING TO DO!

DON'T PANIC, STAND STILL, DON'T PANIC, STAND STILL, DON'T PANIC, STAND STILL . . ."

Over and over she repeated it, and gradually, the other cheerleaders took up the cry. It seemed like forever, but perhaps it was only a minute before the crowd seemed to be stopping, seemed to be less like cattle in a cattle car and more like people in control of their senses.

Then the lights went out.

Now the flames could be seen, licking up the

far wall. The smoke suddenly became thicker, as thick and suffocating as the dark.

"We're all going to be killed!" shrieked Marla.

And then Delle saw it.

High on the catwalk above the gym, a lone figure stood etched against the flames.

Coach Truite.

Chapter 23

"You're going to die!" she howled. "You're all going to DIE!" And she began to laugh hysterically.

"No!" cried Delle. She ran toward the back of the gym and scrambled up the bleachers, the heat of the flames scorching her eyebrows, her bangs.

Running behind her, Greg said, almost conversationally, "She's crazy."

"We've got to stop her!" panted Delle. "We've got to make her open those doors."

She pulled up short at the top of the bleachers.

The catwalk hung from the ceiling, impossibly far away. Old and not used anymore the catwalk was no longer connected to any reachable part of the gym.

Trying to steady her voice, trying to be

heard above the terrible sounds below, Delle called, "Coach! Coach Truite!"

The woman on the catwalk turned.

But it was no longer the Coach Truite that Delle had feared and had, yes, even come to admire and respect. The woman who stood on the catwalk was no longer neat and organized and precise and pulled together.

No. It was as if she was coming to pieces, breaking apart before their very eyes.

The neat black hair stood out wildly around her head. Her eyes were burning black holes in her ash-smudged, ghastly white face. Her lips were drawn back and bloody where she kept biting them, as if gnashing her teeth.

"Coach," said Delle desperately.

Slowly, slowly, Coach Truite turned her head.

"Coach, how do we open the doors? Tell me," said Delle, trying to make her voice sound calm and reasonable.

Coach Truite smiled. It was a terrible sight to see.

"You don't," she said, her voice matching Delle's. "All week I've been torturing you — starting that little fire in your room — I was just practicing . . . that lovely little doll in Susan's room . . . rigging up the equipment to break just at the right moment . . ." the coach cackled with glee. "And now the grand finale. You're all going to die."

Abruptly the smile left her face. "You all deserve to die."

Behind her, Delle heard Greg say so quietly that she wasn't even sure she heard him herself, "The rope."

And she realized that there was a length of rope attached to the catwalk, and looped over a ring high on the wall above the bleachers.

High enough for Greg to reach? To swing out to the swaying, shuddering catwalk?

Delle forced herself not to think about it. She had to keep Coach Truite's attention.

"Why?" she asked. "Why are you doing this?"

"Don't you know?" The coach's eyes widened as if she were genuinely puzzled. "Don't you understand?"

"Tell me," pleaded Delle.

"He died. I raised him, you see. He was the only family I had."

"Who died?"

"Reginald," said the coach, suddenly angry.

"I'm sorry, I don't understand."

"He was my brother. My little baby brother. He was a cheerleader here . . ."

"Reginald Trout," said Delle, remembering

the list of names that had been read out.

"Yes," said the coach. "I taught him gymnastics. I taught him everything. And then he came here. I didn't want him to leave. I didn't want him to go away. It isn't safe out there, I told him.

"But he left me anyway.

"And then he was killed. So I came here. To punish. To pay back. To make you all suffer as he suffered."

"It was an accident," said Delle. "A terrible accident. Nothing can change that. Why punish *us*? Why punish the cheerleaders?"

"Because I hate you. I HATE YOU. I hate you all, stupid cheerleaders in your stupid uniforms. IHATEYOUIHATEYOU. . . ."

"Please,"said Delle. "Please don't do this. Please help us!"

From behind her, without warning, Greg launched himself at the rope. Caught it. Slipped. Caught it again. And began to swing in an agonizingly slow arc above the gym, in and out of the flickering light of the flames like a scene from an old, old movie.

And then he'd caught the edge of the catwalk a few feet behind the coach.

"Coach!" Delle cried, trying to keep her attention.

But it was no use. Coach Truite whirled

around. Strode forward and stood above Greg who'd let go of the rope and was trying with all his might to hoist himself up on the catwalk.

Coach Truite looked down. Smiled.

"You can die first," she said and raised her foot to kick Greg off the catwalk, to send him falling, falling, to the flames below.

"NOOOO," screamed Delle. "NOOO. . . ."

Something red seared Delle's eyes, her brain.

And then Coach Truite stumbled back. She threw up her hands, her own voice a twisted, terrified echo of Delle's.

"NO!" she pleaded. "NO! Stay away from me! NO!"

Frozen, Delle watched in horror as Coach Truite swayed sickeningly on the narrow catwalk.

And then, without warning, without a sound, fell down into the flames.

Chapter 24

She's dead, thought Delle. *And now we're all going to die.*

But even as the flames seemed to engulf the wall, the sound of sirens could be heard outside. A moment later, the doors to the gym burst open and the lights came on. Firefighters poured into the building and attacked the flames. They surged over them, subduing them, putting them out, shepherding the panicked crowd safely from the gym.

Numbly, Delle watched it all from above.

Numbly, she watched Greg scramble down the huge ladder the firefighters brought into the gym.

Numbly, she allowed herself to be helped down from the smoky heights of the bleachers and out into the blissful smokefree air of the night.

She stood, wrapped in a blanket, watching

the others being helped by paramedics and fire-fighters and police officers.

"Looks like only one casualty," she heard one firefighter say. "It's a miracle."

And maybe it was at that, thought Delle, remembering what she had seen up on the catwalk.

Greg's voice, raspy with smoke, had never sounded so good. "You're okay?"

She nodded. She allowed him to pull her against him hard. How had she ever doubted him?

"It was her," said Delle. "Coach Truite."

"I heard. Her little brother."

Delle nodded. "How she must have hated us. He was all she ever had."

"She never *had* him," said Greg. "You can't own anybody. The only way to keep someone is to know when to let 'em go."

Delle laughed weakly. "I'm in no condition to debate that now."

"Yeah, I guess not. Still . . . to blame *us* for her brother's death . . ."

"Maybe she was always crazy," suggested Delle. "Maybe his death was what pushed her over the edge."

She shuddered, remembering all that had happened. "She did all of it. That's why she was always able to be right there. She watched you and me go into the gym that night, and then came back and 'caught' us."

"And she had master keys to Abbey House. It was easy for her to slip into your room, and into Susan's," Greg said.

Delle nodded. "And she was always roaming around, doing curfew checks and stuff. That's probably why she wanted us all in Abbey House. So she could torture us. Make us suffer the way she imagined her brother suffered."

"The Lady in Red won't have the gym to haunt anymore, now," said Greg, looking at the blazing fire consuming the building.

"Maybe she won't need to," said Delle softly. She was remembering something: the night of the fire in her room. The ghost had awakened her.

And the fire hadn't spread. Because the windows of her room had been closed.

Delle shuddered slightly, remembering the icy coldness of her room in spite of the fire. The icy coldness of the doorknob.

What had Mojo said? The chill in the air was the manifestation of a ghost.

A ghost who wasn't a messenger of death, but trying to save a life?

And what about that scream, the scream only Delle had heard, the day the backboard had fallen.

Had that been the Lady in Red, too?

By the fiery blaze of the dying gym, Delle looked up into Greg's face intently. Had he seen what she had seen, up there on the catwalk?

"Did you see her?" Delle asked.

Greg frowned slightly. "Coach Truite? Yeah. She was out of it. I don't think she even knew what was happening at the end, when she slipped off the catwalk."

No. Greg hadn't seen.

He hadn't seen her. The Lady in Red. A thin and wavering figure, sad and lonely, high on the catwalk above the flames. Appearing one last time to save Greg's life, and Delle's, and everybody's.

"She's at peace now," said Delle softly. And she knew it was true. The Lady in Red wouldn't have to haunt this world anymore.

Greg's arm tightened around Delle.

"Let's get out of here," he said.

"Yes," said Delle. "Yes."

We were all such good friends. Who would have thought it would turn out like this?

It's her fault. She's responsible. And she knows it, no matter what she says. No wonder she's so messed up. Forgetting things, losing things, driving too fast, getting into trouble on and off campus . . . if that's not a guilty conscience, what is?

We all know she's guilty. We pretend we don't, but the truth is there, lying among us, like something rotting. She took something precious from us, and we're all pretending it's okay.

But it's not okay. How could it be? She hasn't been punished.

That's not right. Not right at all.

Something had to be done.

She was given a fair hearing, by the only one of us with guts enough to do it. All of the evidence was weighed carefully. And when that was done, there really was no other choice. She had to be convicted. Because she was guilty. No question about it.

And now the sentence has to be carried-out. That's the way justice works, right? Of course, there was only one possible sentence . . .

The death penalty.

Maybe the execution should take place at Nightmare Hall. What could be more perfect? It certainly looks like executions would take place there. Like a prison . . . all that dark brick and those creepy old trees, their black branches hanging down like a hangman's rope. And we've all heard the stories about what happened there . . .

Yes, Nightmare Hall is the perfect place. Perfect. . . .

About the Author

"Writing tales of horror makes it hard to convince people that I'm a nice, gentle person," says **Diane Hoh**.

"So what's a nice woman like me doing scaring people?

"Discovering the fearful side of life: what makes the heart pound, the adrenalin flow, the breath catch in the throat. And hoping always that the reader is having a frightfully good time, too."

Diane Hoh grew up in Warren, Pennsylvania. Since then, she has lived in New York, Colorado, and North Carolina, before settling in Austin, Texas. "Reading and writing take up most of my life," says Hoh, "along with family, music, and gardening." Her other horror novels include *Funhouse*, *The Accident*, *The Invitation*, *The Fever*, and *The Train*.

THRILLERS

Nobody Scares 'Em Like R.L. Stine

☐	BAJ44236-8	The Baby-sitter	$3.50
☐	BAJ44332-1	The Baby-sitter II	$3.50
☐	BAJ46099-4	The Baby-sitter III	$3.50
☐	BAJ45386-6	Beach House	$3.50
☐	BAJ43278-8	Beach Party	$3.50
☐	BAJ43125-0	Blind Date	$3.50
☐	BAJ43279-6	The Boyfriend	$3.50
☐	BAJ44333-X	The Girlfriend	$3.50
☐	BAJ45385-8	Hit and Run	$3.25
☐	BAJ46100-1	Hitchhiker	$3.50
☐	BAJ43280-X	The Snowman	$3.50
☐	BAJ43139-0	Twisted	$3.50

Available wherever you buy books, or use this order form.

Scholastic Inc., P.O. Box 7502, 2931 East McCarty Street, Jefferson City, MO 65102

Please send me the books I have checked above. I am enclosing $_____ (please add $2.00 to cover shipping and handling). Send check or money order — no cash or C.O.D.s please.

Name _____ Birthdate _____

Address _____

City _____ State/Zip _____

Please allow four to six weeks for delivery. Offer good in the U.S. only. Sorry, mail orders are not available to residents of Canada. Prices subject to change
RLS193

WARNING Thrillers by **Diane Hoh** contain irresistible ingredients which may be hazardous to your peace of mind!

☐BAP44330-5	**The Accident**	$3.25
☐BAP45401-3	**The Fever**	$3.25
☐BAP43050-5	**Funhouse**	$3.25
☐BAP44904-4	**The Invitation**	$3.25
☐BAP45640-7	**The Train**	$3.25

Available wherever you buy books, or use this order form.